Time Whisperer

The Journey of a Healer

Meenaa

Copyright © 2024 Meena Bisht

Made with ❤ on the Notion Press Platform

www.notionpress.com

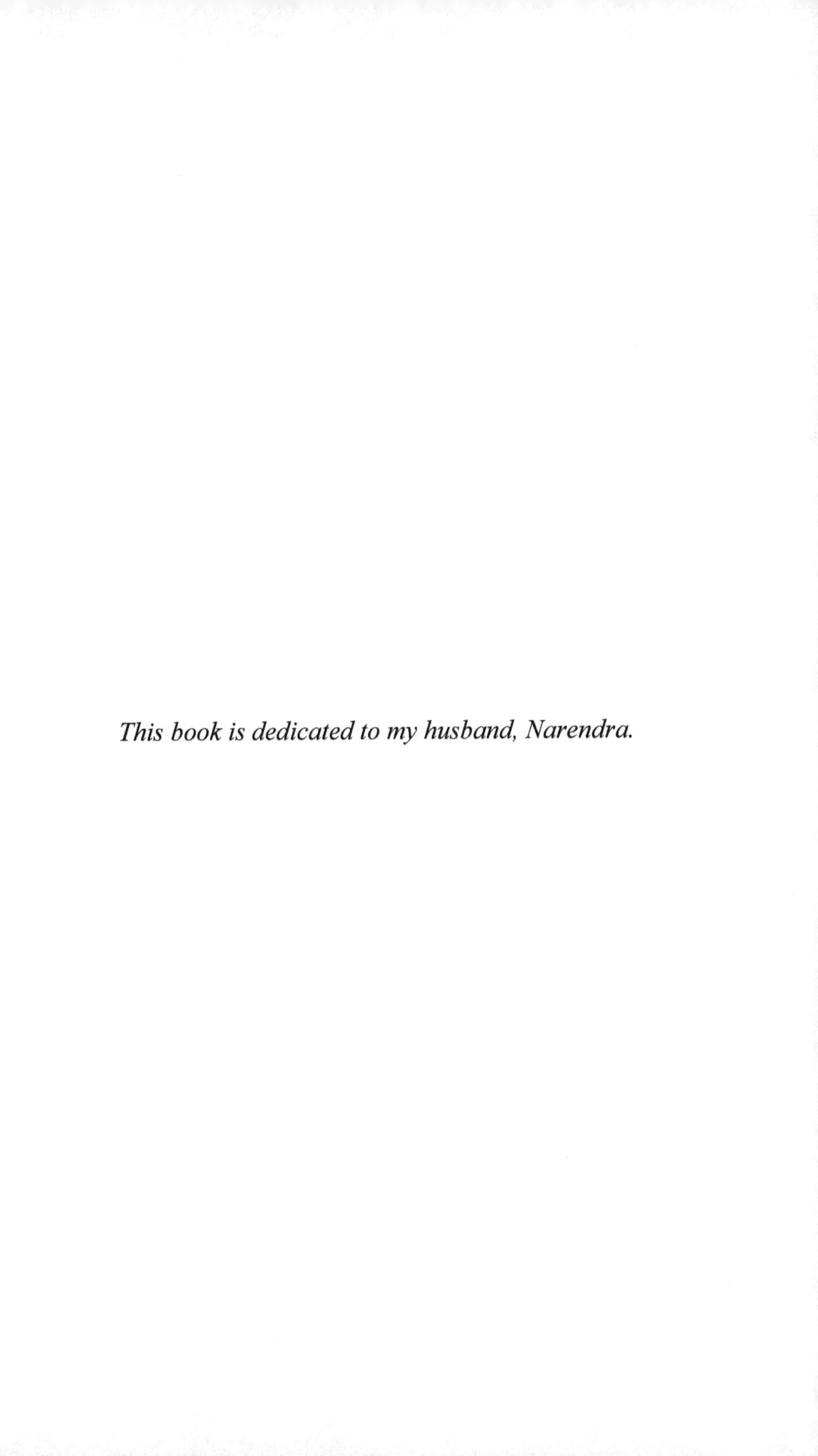

This book is dedicated to my husband, Narendra.

Contents

Foreword .... *vii*

Preface .... *ix*

Acknowledgments .... *xi*

Chapter 1 15

Chapter 2 16

Chapter 3 19

Chapter 4 21

Chapter 5 25

Chapter 6 27

Chapter 7 38

Chapter 8 40

Chapter 9 42

Chapter 10 51

Chapter 11 54

Chapter 12 58

Chapter 13 62

Chapter 14 70

Chapter 15 71

Chapter 16 74

Chapter 17 76

Chapter 18 80

Chapter 19 86

Chapter 20 91

Chapter 21 103

CONTENTS

Chapter 22 120

Chapter 23 124

Chapter 24 128

Chapter 25 129

Chapter 26 135

Chapter 27 140

Chapter 28 144

Chapter 29 146

Chapter 30 157

Chapter 31 161

Chapter 32 168

Chapter 33 170

Foreword

It is with immense pleasure that I write this foreword for Time Whisperer, the debut novel by the multifaceted and immensely talented Meenaa. A home-maker turned spiritual explorer, Meenaa brings her vast experiences as a tarot reader, Akashic healer, numerologist, psychologist, yoga instructor, and dance teacher into the fabric of this fascinating tale.

At its heart, Time Whisperer is the journey of Mira, a healer and past-life regression therapist, who navigates the unseen dimensions of existence with courage and grace. Through Mira's eyes, we are invited to explore the profound mysteries of the universe—questions of karma, soul connections, and the timeless threads binding our lives together. The narrative beautifully balances Mira's spiritual awakening with deeply human experiences, creating a story that is both mystical and relatable.

Meenaa's ability to weave her own curiosity and wisdom into this narrative is what makes Time Whisperer truly special. As a debut author, her writing resonates with authenticity, encouraging readers to reflect on their own lives and spiritual journeys.

This book is not just a story—it is an invitation to explore the vast dimensions of our being. Meenaa has gifted us with a narrative that is both enlightening and deeply moving.

Gautam Patel

Breatharian, Marathon Runner, Writer

23/11/2024

Preface

As an author, I have always been fascinated by the mysteries of existence—the threads that bind us to our past, the whispers of the universe that guide us, and the immense potential for transformation within every soul. Time Whisperer is born from this curiosity, weaving together my personal journey and the imagined world of Mira, the story's protagonist.

Mira is a healer, a seeker, and a bridge between realms. Her journey is deeply spiritual yet rooted in universal human experiences—love, loss, resilience, and redemption. Through her ability to navigate dimensions and touch the souls of others, she invites us to question the nature of time, karma, and the ties that connect us to the eternal.

This story was not written in a vacuum. As a home-maker, tarot reader, Akashic healer, numerologist, psychologist, yoga instructor, and dance teacher, I have drawn from my own experiences to give depth to Mira's character and the world she inhabits. These roles have not just shaped me; they have also shaped the narrative, infusing it with authenticity and insight.

Writing Time Whisperer was an exploration, an unveiling of the unseen. It was also deeply personal—a way of channelling my curiosity about Vedic astrology, metaphysics, and the mysteries of the soul. Mira's story reflects my belief that life is more than what we see; it is a dance of energies, a journey through lifetimes, and a discovery of purpose.

I hope that as you delve into this book, it resonates with you not just as a reader but as a seeker. Let Mira's journey inspire you to explore your own, to embrace the unknown, and to listen to the whispers of time within your soul.

Meenaa

23/11/2024

Acknowledgments

I am grateful to my son, Pranav, for his technical and practical support. I also thank my husband for his unwavering encouragement. My heartfelt appreciation goes to Cpt. Preetham Madhukar, whose advice and patient guidance gave me the confidence and clarity to start writing a story so close to my heart. I am fortunate to have friends like Gautam Patel and Anu Agarwal, who have supported and encouraged me throughout my writing journey. Lastly, I extend my gratitude to my clients and students, who have been instrumental in my spiritual and intellectual growth.

Chapter 1

In a realm, where the veil between the past, present and future was thin, she, a curious soul, was hovering above from far to unknown, uncanny places and people, drawing to the mysteries of her own heart. She always felt, there is much more to explore, much more to express. This knowledge flowed in her veins. She just knew it. Sky painted with stars, she was visiting a wise old lady, known as the Tarot Lady. The Tarot Lady's dimly lit abode, filled with the faint scent of incense and the glow of flickering candles, seemed like a portal to another realm. She was renowned for her abilities to read cards and unveil the secrets of the soul. Dimly lit rooms, scent of incense filled the air and flickering candlelight danced upon the wall, casting shadows that seemed to tell their own stories.

"Welcome dear child. What brings you to my humble abode"? Her voice was like a soothing melody. "I seek to understand the desires and talents from the deep pit of my heart." Mira replied and her eyes sparkling with anticipation. "I wish to know how they shape my present and guide my future."

The Tarot Lady smiled knowingly and gestured to Mira to sit at the table adorned with a vibrant tapestry. She shuffled the tarot deck, the cards whispering secrets as they moved. With a gentle flick of her wrist, she laid off three cards. The Wheel of Fortune, the High Priestess and the Star.

"The Wheel of Fortune," the Tarot Lady began, her voice steady and serene, "represents the cycles of life and the lessons we carry from one existence to another. It speaks of a past life where you experienced both triumph and hardship, each shaping the person you are today." Mira leaned closer, her pulse quickening as warmth spread through her chest. The Tarot Lady continued, her wise eyes gleaming under the dim candlelight. As the Tarot Lady placed the next card before Mira, her gaze softened, hinting at deeper revelations. "The High Priestess signifies your innate intuition and connection to the spiritual realm. In past lives, you were a healer, a guide—someone who unravelled the mysteries of the universe. This wisdom is your gift, waiting to be embraced." Hearing the Tarot Lady's words, Mira's heart quickened. The thought of having been a healer in a past life sent a shiver down her spine—was this the answer she had been seeking all along?"

As she turned to the final card, Mira's heart fluttered with hope. "And, The Star," the Tarot Lady said, her smile soft but knowing, "is your beacon of hope and inspiration. Your talents are not mere remnants of the past; they are the guiding light for your future. Embrace them, and you will shine brightly in this life."

With each word, Mira felt a wave of clarity wash over her, as though the shadows of her doubts were retreating. The Tarot Lady's insights illuminated her path, revealing that her past lives were not just echoes of history but powerful influences guiding her journey.

Inspired, Mira left the Tarot Lady's abode, her heart brimming with purpose.

Chapter 2

The alarm rang on Mira's mobile. Mira's mobile alarm shattered the fragile silence of dawn, pulling her from the depths of a strange and vivid dream. What kind of dream she just had! All these symbols, scenarios or people in the dream hold clues to something in her present realities.

She was sensing an entity, with the energy of a guide or guardian; energy, protective yet enigmatic. She just looked with closed eyes inside herself and felt like a bottomless pot, a feeling that was ready to take her to mysterious journeys. She just had to surrender herself to the will of this weirdness which seems separate from her. And in these quiet moments of dawn, she was reflecting on the wisdom of the Tarot Lady from her vivid dream, knowing that the talents of her pasts were forever a part of her, illuminating her path in this life and beyond.

There is no substitute for hard work and experience. Mira not only knew it but embraced it as a mantra to move ahead in her tarot cards reading & healing journey. Countless nights found Mira hunched over her tarot cards, studying their patterns and energies. Every reading, every moment of self-reflection, was a step forward in her journey of mastery. Mira poured herself into her craft, each reading sharpening her intuition. And now after many moons, under the soft glow of flickering candles, her sacred space awaited a round table, draped in deep purple velvet, sitting in the centre. On it an intricately designed deck of cards lay waiting, as if alive with unseen energy.

Candles flickered gently, casting soft golden light around the room, while the scent of lavender incense danced in the air. The room had become a crossroads of realms, where clients from various walks of life—human, celestial and otherworldly — sought out the guidance of Time Whisperer.

Her reputation was spreading far and wide, reaching realms she had never imagined, from mystical forests, bustling cities and even the ethereal lands beyond the human world. Individuals arriving with hopes, fears and unanswered questions. She welcomed them all, no matter their age, background, or form. With each reading, she became a vessel for the stories of others, unravelling their pasts, interpreting their presents and guiding them toward their futures. The cards were her sacred tool, each one imbued with its own unique power. As she shuffled the deck, the energy in the room shifted and she could feel the presence of her next client approaching.

It was a typical early evening in her home. The smell of dinner—simple daal, and fried spicy aloo. The living room was softly illuminated by the warm glow of a single lamp, casting gentle shadows against the walls dotted with family photographs. Ingredients for dinner simmering on the stove, filling the air with enticing aromas of cumin and coriander. Outside, the sun was beginning to set, painting the sky in hues of orange, pink and purple, while the first stars began to twinkle into existence, Mira with an aura of mystique, set cross legged on the floor, her vibrant sari was flowing around her like a colourful tapestry. She had always been a woman of deep thoughts and spirited discussions, her dark eyes reflecting a curiosity for the wisdom of the universe. Her gaze drifted to the window where the sky was now a canvas of fading light, stars slowly emerging to offer their silent witness to her silent thoughts.

She started remembering the time when celestial entities started to become more and more apparent to her. She was in Uttarakhand, where she went to spend some time alone to meditate and write, and there something happened which shifted something inside herself, as if mountains had unlocked an unseen doorway in her soul.

Chapter 3

As the sun was about to dip behind the Himalayas, casting long, purple shadows over the peaks. Mira strolled down a narrow path just behind her cabin. The air was crisp with the scent of pine and earth. It had rained earlier that day, leaving the leaves glistening in the fading light. The only sounds were her gentle humming and the occasional rustle of the forest until she heard something more. The path she walked was framed by tall trees whose gnarled branches stretched out like ancient arms, creating a canopy overhead. The further she walked, the quieter the world seemed as though nature itself was holding its breath. She reached a small clearing, lit only by the dim light of the twilight, when she felt an overwhelming presence.

Standing there was a woman, older, but striking. Her hair was flying wild and dark streaked with silver and her eyes appeared dark black glowing slightly in the dim light. She wore a long flowing black robe made from what looked like threads of the night sky itself. Around her neck, hung a talisman of bone and obsidian, and her bare feet seemed barely touching the earth beneath her.

 This was Kali, an ancient witch, but not in a way folklore might suggest. There was something modern, almost timeless about her. The air around her seemed to hum with energy. Both ancient and new. Mira froze, her heart pounding, but not out of fear instead a strange calmness washed over her as if she had known this woman for lifetimes. Kali's voice when she spoke was soft yet powerful. Each word wrapping around Mira, like a protective embrace.

"You have come far, little writer." She said her eyes were twinkling, "and yet this journey is just beginning." Kali then guided Mira deeper into the forest where the trees grew even older, their trunk thick with moss and the air was thick with magic. They stopped at a stone altar weathered with time, but still radiating power here. Kali told her story how she had once been a woman like Mira, seeking purpose only to discover her gifts. She had spent centuries mastering the elements, guiding lost souls, and weaving the threads of destiny. Kali shared her rituals, revealing small gestures that control the wind, the rain, and the very pulse of the Earth. She showed Mira how to call upon the spirits of the forest, how to meditate and draw power from the moon and how to get rid of fear. The two women sat in quiet contemplation as they performed a ritual calling on the stars above them.

Light dimmed and for a moment, the world felt like it was holding its breath, time stopped. Mira watched in awe as Kali chanted softly. The air around her shimmering. With life and energy. The ritual wasn't for power or control, it was for gratitude, a thank you to the Earth for all it had given. As they shared their final moments, Kali embraced Mira and though no words were spoken, there was an understanding between them— a passing of wisdom, strength and purpose. Tears welled in both their eyes not of sorrow, but of joy and connection.

At first, it was subtle—a brush of cool air against her cheek in an otherwise warm room, the sudden urge to turn her head to catch a movement just at the edge of her vision. She dismissed these oddities thinking they were merely echoes of her time in solitude, remnants of the serene and sometimes eerie energy that had surrounded her in the mountains. But soon these fleeting sensations become something more, much more. It started with whispers, faint at first, like a distant murmur carried on the wind. They floated through her dreams and seeped into her waking moments. It was no longer just a sensation; it was the presence. Mira could feel them around her. Different types of energies are no longer vague or formless, as they had been before, these presences took on shapes indistinct yet palpable. They were not human but felt human in their stories, in their longing, their Joy and their pain.

Chapter 4

One evening while sitting at her kitchen table, Mira felt a deep chill crawl up her spine but it wasn't the cold that startled her. It was the feeling that she wasn't alone and this time it was undeniable. She turned and there standing by the window, was a figure not solid, not fully formed, but a shimmering sense of light and shadow. It didn't speak at first, but Mira felt a wave of emotion crash over her. Raw and aching—and a surge of sorrow that wasn't her own. "What? Who are you?" She asked, her voice trembling. No words came out but in her mind. Mira felt the response. *I have been waiting. I have been forgotten.* A flood of images flashed through her mind.

A boy of 10-11 years old looking frustrated as he was unable to speak directly and convey his story to others was adding to his despair. This was where Mira came in, gifted with the ability to hear whispers across time & dimensions. She immediately started drawing her cards to guide his soul, helping him understand that he is known and he could release his anger. Through a healing ritual, Mira performed an energy cleansing, and with her compassionate guidance, Madhav's spirit found the courage to express itself. Mira was feeling a rush of emotions— fear, confusion and of course frustration. The ghost child's memories wash over her like waves, vivid yet haunting. Madhav appeared to her as a faint image: a small boy with expressive eyes, dressed in tattered, traditional clothing, holding onto a small toy made of wood that reminded him of his happier times. Mira's heart ached for him as she realized his soul was trapped in a loop of suffering, replaying his final moments over and over again.

He lost his life in a very tragic way. One moment playing with his friends in a pond just outside the village, another moment got stuck and tangled in thick, muddy weeds beneath the water. They held him tight, tightening as he struggled. The murky water swallowed his frantic cries for help, muffling his pleas. Madhav's friends initially laughed and thought he was just playing, as they saw him struggling, his hands flailing above the water's surface. But they were too young, too scared, their laughter fading into horror as they watched helplessly.

Underneath, Madhav's vision blurred, the sunlight filtering through the water in fractured ways. His chest burned as he fought to break free. Every movement became slower as his energy waned. His mind raced with confusion and terror; he couldn't understand why this was happening. In those final moments, he thought of his mother, his home. The simple joys he would never experience aga

in as his body went still. The pond returned to its quiet state. The water calmed once more, betraying no sign of the life that had been lost. The pond remained silent, holding his memory within its depths, a place he would be forever bound to, until Mira's compassion reached him across time, to reach the core of Madhav's suffering. Mira decided to access a realm where all thoughts, actions and Karmic imprints are stored. These records, these Akashic records held the answers. She needed to understand Madhav's pain and to find a way to free him.

Entering this ethereal library was a sacred process. One Mira approaches with reverence, preparing herself with meditation and centring exercises. To alleviate her consciousness, she lit a candle in an otherwise dark room. She sat on a soft cushion, palms facing upward, eyes gently closed. She held a clear quartz crystal, believed to heighten connection and whispered a prayer to open the records, asking for permission to enter and seek guidance for Madhav. Her consciousness was expanding and she felt his spirit. Transported to a vast boundless space, filled with glowing streams of light, each one representing a soul's journey across lifetime. The energy shifts as Mira's intent sharpened. Focused especially on Madhav, as she delved deeper, she encountered a faint shimmer—the essence of the young boy. Mira looked deeper, she sensed many layers of his suffering, a karmic bond from many prior lifetimes. Mira Guided by this knowledge, now called upon her healing powers to release Madhav from his karmic entanglement. She visualized a radiant light enveloping his soul, gently unrevealing the bonds that held him to his pasts. She spoke aloud declaring the lessons which the divine wanted him to learn. Madhav accepted every suggestion given by Mira. He slowly, consciously surrendered every conditioning, fear, frustration. He felt tremendous agility & lightness. His soul was getting healed from a painful death experience, breaking the cycle that had trapped him for so long.

In the quiet of her room Mira faced a profound shift, Madhav's spirit appeared to her calmer and brighter. She told him that he was ready to go to higher realms and that he no longer needed to linger in this plane. With tears in his eyes, Madhav finally accepted his release he had been longing for. As the energy softened, Mira watched Madhav's spirit ascend, merging into the light of the Akashic divine field, where he would find peace and healing. She closed the records with a sense of reverence, whispering her gratitude to the spirit guides, for helping her to bring resolution to this young soul. The room fell into silence.

Mira sensed an immense peace spreading across her senses and body.

Mira carefully shuffled her well-worn deck, each card infused with her energy and intent. She is looking for final closure. The last advice from the heavens. She closed her eyes, centred herself and silently asked the divine guidance to reconfirm that Madhav's soul had truly been released and the cards revealed themselves, forming a story before her.

The first card revealed the Judgement, a powerful symbol of liberation echoing the release that Madhav's soul is moving through a phase of rebirth. Free from the bonds of the earthly realm, ascending toward a new journey. The second card is the Ace of Cups, a symbol of emotional peace overflowing with divine energy. It spoke to her about the tranquillity that awaits both Madhav and herself. Mira understood that this card is heaven's acknowledgement of her selfless act, a reminder that her compassion has opened the path for peace. Then Hierophant emerges, a symbol of her calling and a knowledge she had. This card resonated deeply, reminding Mira of a higher purpose. It signified that her journey as a healer is far from over, that she must use her gifts with renewed dedication and respect for the responsibilities.

Mira placed her hands over the cards, feeling the energy pulse through her. After the Hierophant, Mira drew two more cards that deepened her understanding of the message from heaven. The Star appeared symbolizing hope, guidance and divine clarity. This card radiated a gentle light that seemed to reach Mira's soul. Reminding her that she is not alone in this fascinating journey. The Star represented her connection to divine wisdom, reinforcing her faith and commitment to healing. It is also a sign that Mira's journey will continue to be illuminated by divine grace, guiding her to help others find peace, just as she got with Madhav finally. The Six of Swords emerged, showing a figure moving from turbulent waters towards calm shores. This card reflected Mira's journey of helping souls transition from unrest to peace. It told her that her role as a healer would often require guiding others through painful transformations, much like her experience with Madhav's release. The Six of Swords is both a message for herself and a reminder of the support she provided to those who seek her healing touch.

Mira reflected on these cards, feeling a profound understanding of her purpose, The Star and Six of Swords confirmed that she is meant to be a guide for others, shining the light in the darkness and helping them across, from suffering into serenity, the sense of responsibility, love and happiness deepened within her, knowing she is on the right path. At this moment she knew she had received confirmation from heaven. Warmth filled her heart and with it an unshakable sense of self-worth.

Chapter 5

Mira's journey into the world of the unseen was not just an unsettling awakening, it was to get her to her spiritual transformation. Each interaction with these entities, each immersion into their stories was more than an encounter. It was a lesson, a piece of a puzzle that revealed a greater understanding of life. Death and the infinite realities that lay beyond the physical world. At first, Mira had been afraid about the weight of the entities' emotions and the vividness of their stories. It all overwhelmed her, but over time something began to shift. With every encounter, her fear began to dissolve, replaced by a deep curiosity and a sense of purpose in each entity. She communicated with them whether they were silent and angry or peaceful, offering her an unspoken gift, a new layer of insight into the spiritual realm.

These interactions sharpened her intuition. She started noticing that certain energies carried distinct frequencies. She could sense which spirits were attached to places like old houses or forgotten roads and which ones followed her, seeking her out because they knew she could hear them. It was as if her internal compass had been recalled, attuned not to the world of the living but to the many layers of existence beyond it. With every spirit she encountered, Mira began to understand that she was not just a passive listener but an active participant in their release, their journey. By acknowledging them, by hearing their stories, she was helping these lost energies find closure, giving them a chance to move on. And in doing so, she herself was becoming more attuned to the spiritual laws that governed the unseen as she grew stronger in her spiritual awakening. Sometimes she wondered if it was her writing, her way of capturing the essence of life in words, that called to them. Perhaps these spirits, these entities, sort out because she could give voice to their silenced stories, their fleeting existence into permanence. Or maybe it was something deeper, something she had yet to understand.

The line between the two, her reality and theirs had blurred, and Mira couldn't tell where one ended and the other began. But even though it terrified her at times even though she wanted to shut it all out, she knew she couldn't. There was a pull, a compulsion, a need to listen, to witness. Their stories—these echoes of forgotten lives—had found her for a reason and Mira knew she had to carry on, no matter how painful they became. As days were passing Mira, feeling stronger in her spiritual awareness, she began experiencing something even more profound- An ability to slip between dimensions. It happened one evening. When she was sitting in meditation, a practice, she had started regularly after her return from Uttarakhand. Her breathing slowed and so did her mind. She felt her consciousness loosen, as if her body was no longer a boundary but a vessel. She could leave at will. Suddenly, the room around her seemed to melt away. The world around her, the furniture faded, and she found herself standing in a vast open space, illuminated via a soft otherworldly light. It wasn't a place in the physical sense. There were no solid structures, no ground beneath her feet, but it was undeniably real. Here, the air hummed with a quiet energy, and Mira could feel the presence of countless beings around her. Some were the same entities she had spoken to before, but there were other energies too. In this dimension, time felt different, as if it stretched out infinitely and contracted all at once. Mira understood that here, past, present, in future were not separate but layered, coexisting in ways the human mind couldn't fully comprehend.

It was in this place that she began to realize her own soul was much more expansive than she had ever imagined. She could feel parts of herself in different times and places, existing in other forms, and living out different experiences. Her first journey into this dimension was brief, a glimpse that left her shaken, but exhilarated. With each subsequent meditation Mira found it easier to return. The transition became smoother, and soon she learned how to move between this dimension and her everyday life with more ease. She no longer feared losing herself in these spaces; instead, she embraced them as opportunities to explore the vastness of her own consciousness.

Chapter 6

In the dim glow of a late autumn afternoon, Mira stepped into the quaint little café on the corner, drawn by the scent of fresh-brewed coffee and the warmth that promised respite from the world outside. The gentle hum of soft music played in the background, mingling with the scent of fresh coffee and pastries. She'd only come to escape the weight of her thoughts, but as she entered, she noticed him—a man who seemed known, though she'd never seen him before.

He sat by the window, framed in the soft light that spilled through, casting him in an otherworldly aura. He looked like no ordinary man; his presence was soothing, like a shadow woven with silk, barely tethered to the earth. He wore an ageless expression—a quiet, that stirred Mira's curiosity and an elegance that made him seem like he belonged to another time, another place.

He was drawing glances from everyone around, though he appeared completely unaware of it. His hair was long, the kind of dark, midnight-black that hinted at mystery, falling in waves past his shoulders and framing his sharp, striking features. His skin had a sun-kissed warmth, though there was a natural glow to it, as if he spent his time absorbing something far beyond mere sunlight.

His eyes were pools of uncharted mysteries, ancient yet alight with childlike wonder, deep-set and smouldering, were an intense shade of chestnut flecked with amber, carrying both a sense of ancient wisdom and an untamed fire. They were the kind of eyes that, once they locked onto you, held you in place, unravelling layers with a single look. A touch of stubble dusted his jawline, giving him a rugged edge that contrasted beautifully with the elegance of his high cheekbones and perfectly arched brows. His lips, neither too full nor too thin, curved naturally into an expression of quiet confidence, as if they held secrets he wouldn't easily reveal.

His frame was lean, yet his build hinted at strength—muscles defined enough to show through his fitted attire, but without any pretence. He wore a loose, charcoal-coloured linen shirt that draped over his torso, open just enough at the collar to reveal the smooth, inviting skin at the base of his neck. His fingers, long and elegant, rested around his glass of water with a grace that spoke of control, of calm, yet they hinted at an intensity beneath the surface.

There was a paradox to him—a sensual magnetism cloaked in quiet serenity, as if he was a storm contained in a tranquil sea. And when he moved, every gesture was deliberate, as though he understood the weight of his presence, yet chose to carry it lightly. He carried within him the quiet of far-off mountaintops, the hush of dawn over ancient forests.

Suddenly she saw him approaching her. Her heart started fluttering as his presence was becoming denser and denser. Her fingers were playing with the rim of the coffee cup. He stood just a few feet away, his eyes already fixed on her. Tall and composed, he exuded a quiet, calming presence that somehow seemed larger than the room itself. His face held an expression of serene curiosity, as though he'd been searching for something or someone and had finally found it. She felt an odd pull, a familiarity she couldn't place, and before she could look away, he moved towards her table with a gentle, unhurried grace.

"Is this seat taken?" he asked, his voice soft yet resonant, like a whisper that lingered in the air. There was a warmth in his tone, a kindness that disarmed her instinctive caution.

Surprised but intrigued, Mira managed a small smile and shook her head. "No, please," she gestured.

As he settled into the chair across from her, a silence fell between them, yet it wasn't uncomfortable. It felt more like an invitation, a pause rich with something unsaid. He looked at her with a gaze that seemed to reach past her exterior and into something deeper, as though he saw the essence of who she was.

"I'm Atmaj," he said, introducing himself with a nod. "It might sound strange, but I felt drawn to speak with you… as if we were meant to meet."

Mira raised her eyebrows slightly, both taken aback and intrigued by his openness. "Well, Atmaj," she replied, a hint of playfulness in her tone, "that's quite an introduction. I'm Mira. And, yes… somehow, this doesn't feel strange at all."

They shared a quiet smile before he spoke again, his voice gentle and steady. "I sense you're a seeker, Mira. Someone who understands the world beyond what's seen. I find it rare to meet souls with that openness."

She studied him, sensing a profound tranquillity in his presence, as though he was in tune with a rhythm she hadn't quite discovered. "I suppose that's true," she admitted, leaning forward slightly. "I'm a healer… a guide, in a way. I help people understand their own journeys."

He nodded, as if this wasn't surprising in the least. "That explains why your energy feels so familiar," he said thoughtfully. "I, too, am on a path that's taken me beyond the usual bounds of life. I'm what some call a breatharian—someone who finds sustenance not in food, but in the prana, the energy around us." Mira's eyes widened with curiosity. "A breatharian," she repeated softly, as if tasting the word. "I've read about it… but to meet someone who lives this way? That's rare indeed."

They both paused, letting the weight of his words settle between them. Atmaj could feel her curiosity, her readiness to understand, and it made him smile—a smile so calm it felt like a gentle breeze. "It's not an easy path," he explained, "but it has brought me closer to the essence of life. To know oneself as part of the universe, to live without attachments… it's a journey of letting go."

Mira listened intently, her heart beating faster. She had always been drawn to the mystical, to the truths hidden beneath the surface of life, but Atmaj was speaking of a level of freedom she had never dared to imagine. "There's a depth to you," he said softly, as if sensing her thoughts. "Something tells me you're ready to find more of it… if you're open to exploring together."

Mira was caught off guard by his invitation, and she felt the faintest flush of warmth colour her cheeks. But she knew, deep down, that he was right—there was a hunger in her for something more, for a connection beyond the boundaries of everyday existence. "Yes, I would like that," she replied, her voice barely more than a whisper. "I'd like to understand what you see… to learn what it means to live as you do."

Atmaj smiled again, a look of quiet satisfaction crossing his face. "Then perhaps we could meet again, in a week's time? There's a place I know—a peaceful garden tucked away from the noise of the city. We can meet there and continue this conversation." Mira nodded, feeling a strange sense of excitement and calm all at once. "I'd love that," she said, meaning it.

As they stood to leave, he extended his hand to her in a gentle gesture. She took it, feeling the warmth and solidity of his grasp. "Until next time, Mira," he said with a soft, steady gaze that promised much yet asked nothing. "Until then, Atmaj," she replied, her heart strangely full as she watched him walk away, his presence lingering long after he'd disappeared.

That night, as Mira slipped into meditation, she felt herself drawn deeply into a vision—a vivid scene that felt so real, it was as if she had stepped into another time, another place.

She found herself in a small, sun-drenched village, surrounded by fields of golden crops swaying gently in the warm breeze. The air was thick with the earthy scent of soil and ripened wheat. She looked down and saw her bare feet, dusted with the village's reddish-brown soil. Her hands, young and slender, held a woven basket filled with wildflowers. She wore a simple, faded cotton sari, one that spoke of a life of modest means, a life bound to the earth.

In this vision, Mira was no longer the seasoned healer she was today but a young girl, perhaps sixteen. Her heart beat with a quiet, unspoken longing as she glanced up toward a grand house at the far end of the village. It was a sprawling estate, surrounded by tall, ornate gates that seemed out of place amid the humble thatched huts around it. It belonged to Atmaj's family, who was Amar now, the wealthiest and most powerful household in the village.

And there he was—a young man, Amar, not much older than her, leaning against the old Banyan tree that had stood at the edge of the village for as long as anyone could remember. She watched him from afar, her heart stirring as it always did whenever she saw him. Even in this past life, he had that same serene confidence, a light in his eyes that made her feel as though he could see straight through her soul. He was dressed in fine clothes, silk dhoti and kurta, his skin sun-kissed from days spent outdoors, his presence magnetic, commanding yet calm.

Amar noticed her approach, and a soft smile curved his lips. He waved her over, a silent invitation that made her heart flutter. Though they came from different worlds, they had been friends since childhood, drawn to each other in a way that seemed natural, inevitable, as if some invisible thread bound them together despite the gulf between their social standings.

"Are those for me?" he teased gently, glancing at the flowers in her basket as she approached, her cheeks flushing slightly.

Mira hesitated, laughing softly as she looked down at her collection of wild blooms. "Perhaps," she replied, her voice carrying a shyness she couldn't quite conceal. "Though I don't think these would suit a rich man's home."

Amar chuckled, shaking his head. "Nonsense. These are far more beautiful than anything money can buy," he said, his eyes twinkling. "You've always had a way with finding beauty in the simplest things, Radha."

She smiled, her gaze lowering, trying to conceal the longing in her heart. She loved him, with a love that felt as natural as breathing, as inevitable as the seasons. But she knew she couldn't say it. He was Amar, the heir to a powerful family, and she was just the daughter of a poor farmer. She couldn't burden him with her feelings, feelings that could never be returned, not in this life, not with the worlds that separated them.

They spent hours together that day, sitting under the shade of the old oak tree, laughing, talking about their dreams and fears. He spoke of his family's expectations, of the pressure to continue the family legacy, a path that felt increasingly stifling to him. She listened, offering quiet comfort, a presence he could trust. And he, in turn, asked her about her life, about her father's fields and the weight she carried as the only family member left to support him.

They both knew they were drifting toward something forbidden. With every glance, every smile, they grew closer, yet neither dared to cross that invisible line between them.

"Sometimes," he said, his voice soft as a whisper, "I wish things were different, Radha. That we weren't bound by these titles, these walls we didn't build but still live inside."

She looked at him, her heart aching. "If only wishes could change the world," she replied, her voice catching. "But even if they don't, at least we have this—our friendship."

He nodded, though his eyes held a sadness, a yearning that mirrored her own. In that moment, she wanted nothing more than to reach out, to close the distance between them, to tell him that her heart had belonged to him for as long as she could remember.

But before she could speak, a voice called for him from the estate—one of his family's servants, summoning him back to his world of luxury and duty. He looked at her, regret flickering across his face as he stood, brushing the dust from his clothes.

"I'll see you again, Radha," he promised, his voice filled with a quiet intensity. "No matter where life takes us, I'll always find you." And then he was gone, leaving her standing alone under the banyan tree, watching as he disappeared back into his world, one she could never be part of.

The vision faded, and Mira found herself back in her bed, her heart still aching with the bittersweet memory. Her fingers trembled as she touched her cheek, feeling the trace of a tear she hadn't realized had fallen. That young girl, that love unspoken yet enduring, lingered in her mind, filling her with both sorrow and warmth.

Few weeks passed. Radha's world felt like it was slipping away beneath her feet as she made her way to the quiet clearing in the forest. She had arranged to meet Amar here, seeking one last stolen moment together before her marriage. Her heart was heavy, and each step weighed with the knowledge that her life would soon be bound to another man, Viraj—a decision made for her, not by her.

Amar was waiting, leaning against a tree, his face a mixture of confusion, pain, and a love so fierce it seemed to tear him apart. The sight of him sent a sharp ache through Mira's chest, and the air between them was thick with unspoken words. She opened her mouth to speak, but no words came; only silence filled the space, a silence that screamed louder than anything she could say. Amar's eyes were pleading, searching hers, desperate to understand the torment within her.

"Run away with me," he whispered, his voice trembling with a mixture of hope and despair. He reached out, cupping her face in his hands. Mira closed her eyes, feeling the warmth of his touch, her heart fluttering against her ribs as she leaned into him. They stood like that, locked in a timeless embrace, where nothing existed but the intensity of their longing.

Without thinking, he kissed her—soft at first, but then with a desperate hunger that spoke of all they could never have. Mira responded, her hands slipping around his neck, holding onto him as if letting go would mean falling into an abyss. His touch grew more insistent, his lips tracing a path along her jaw, her neck, whispering the depth of his love without words. Mira felt herself surrendering, lost in him, in the freedom they shared away from the world's gaze.

But as his hands slid to her waist, pulling her closer, a voice inside her broke through the haze of passion. She stiffened, drawing back, her eyes filling with tears as she looked up at him.

"No, Amar," she whispered, her voice cracking. "I love you more than words can say, and every part of me wants this… wants you. But I… I can't." Her shoulders began to shake as the weight of their reality sank in. "What we have is sacred, Amar. I cannot taint it, not even for the sake of our love."

Amar's face fell, and he looked at her, pain and frustration twisting his expression. He clenched his fists, swallowing the words he could not say. "Why does it have to be this way?" he asked, his voice barely a whisper. "Why can't we fight this, Mira? Why do you have to be his?"

She bit her lip, tears streaming down her face. "I wish I knew," she said, her voice trembling. "I don't want this life, Amar, but I'm trapped. My father… he has no choice, and now, neither do I."

The two stood in silence, the weight of their impending separation hanging over them like a storm. Finally, as the moonlight filtered through the trees, casting silvery shadows around them, Mira stepped back, looking at him one last time.

"Goodbye, Amar," she said softly, her heart shattering with each word. She turned, walking away with heavy steps, leaving him alone in the darkened forest, his heart filled with anger, loss, and a love that would haunt him forever.

As she lay there, the faint realization dawned on her: this was why she felt such a pull toward Atmaj in this life. It wasn't just the present connection but a thread that had woven through lifetimes. They had found each other before, in different bodies, different circumstances, and though society had kept them apart, the bond between their souls had never broken.

She knew that this time, perhaps, they might have a chance to complete the story, to give voice to the love that had waited, silent yet resilient, through the ages. And as she drifted into sleep, she felt a strange peace, knowing that they were together again, here and now, in this life.

Mira was thrilled about her upcoming session with Atmaj, yet she wrestled with inner doubts and self-reflection. Despite her experience and the strong intuitive abilities, she's cultivated over the years, she sometimes questioned whether she's truly equipped to guide others on such deep, transformative journeys.

Her growing reputation led many new clients scheduling appointments, each with their own unique concerns. One day, she met a woman burdened with anxiety over her son's education and future. The woman spoke about her fears regarding his lack of direction and the uncertainties that lie ahead for him.

Listening intently, Mira offered a calm, reassuring presence, sensing that the woman's anxiety stems partly from her own unresolved fears. To address this, Mira gently guided her to focus on building a nurturing environment where her son can explore his own interests freely. She advised the mother to encourage her son's creativity and individuality, rather than imposing her own aspirations or worries onto him. Mira suggested practical steps: mindful communication, setting realistic expectations, and creating opportunities for the son to express himself.

She also took out her tarot deck, tuning into the energies surrounding the situation. The cards revealed that the son has a unique path ahead, one that may differ from conventional success but holds a deeply fulfilling outcome. Through the reading, Mira assured the woman that her son's journey will align naturally, as long as he's given the space to grow and discover his inner passions. This assured the mother, who left the session with a lighter heart and newfound clarity. Mira, too, felt a sense of fulfilment, knowing she helped someone overcome their fears, even as she continued to wrestle with her own inner questions.

Chapter 7

On the day of their meeting, Mira arrived early at the garden they had chosen, a secluded spot nestled within lush greenery, the kind of place where quiet moments seemed to linger. The late afternoon sun was casting a warm glow over the garden, and a gentle breeze rustled through the leaves. Mira took in the scene, feeling both excitement and nervous anticipation flutter within her.

Aatmaj arrived shortly after, dressed in a simple, well-fitted shirt and dark jeans. He had an air of quiet confidence that Mira found grounding yet intriguing. His gaze met hers as he approached, and they exchanged smiles that conveyed a sense of familiarity, even though they were still uncovering the layers of each other.

They found a bench under an old tree and settled in, the peacefulness of the garden wrapping around them like a blanket. Aatmaj broke the silence first, gently asking about Mira's recent experiences with her clients. Mira shared a few stories, including the mother worried about her son, describing the struggles and emotions that her clients bring to her.

Aatmaj listened intently, his eyes never leaving hers, as if every word she speaks carries a weight he respects. She noticed the way his gaze softened whenever she spoke about her work; it's clear he admired the dedication and empathy she did put into her healing. In turn, Mira asked Aatmaj about his own journey, wanting to know more about the thoughts and experiences that have shaped him.

As the conversation was flowing smoothly, it became clear they share a rare connection—a meeting of souls who have each walked complex paths. They laughed over shared insights, debated spiritual philosophies, and even sat in silence, each absorbed in the presence of the other. With every exchange, their connection deepened, and Mira felt her earlier doubts beginning to fade. She realized that her longing to be with him isn't just attraction but a recognition of the familiar, a sense of unity and mutual respect.

As dusk begins to settle over the garden, they both sensed an unspoken intimacy building between them. The day had slipped by unnoticed, and the once-crowded park was now almost empty. They rose, and Aatmaj reached out, taking her hand gently. She felt a warmth spread from his touch, a feeling both calming and electrifying.

They walked back together in comfortable silence, his hand still in hers, until they reached his place nearby. Without words, they know that they want to spend the night together. There was no rush, no hesitation—just a natural pull, as if this moment had always been meant to happen. They entered his home, a modest yet cozy space filled with warm lighting and shelves lined with books and artifacts from his travels.

In his presence, Mira felt safe yet alive with anticipation. They sat close, and their conversation grew softer, each exchange laden with a deeper meaning. Aatmaj brushed a strand of hair away from Mira's face, his hand lingering as he traced her cheek with his thumb. Their eyes met, and a slow, tender kiss followed—a moment where words were no longer needed.

They moved together with a shared understanding, exploring each other with a sense of reverence and vulnerability. For Mira, it felt like an awakening, a release of all the longing and questions she had carried alone. They made love with a gentle passion, each act imbued with a sense of discovery and trust. Atmaj kissed every part of her with so much reverence and intensity. Touching, kissing, her flower. Beautiful lines, spirals, deep, wet ground to drink from. And in Aatmaj, Mira found a mirror to her own spirit, someone who not only saw her but valued every part of who she was.

As they lay together afterward, Mira rested her head on his chest, feeling his heartbeat steady beneath her. In that peaceful silence, she felt a sense of completeness, as if meeting Aatmaj had unlocked something she didn't realize she was missing. She drifted to sleep, feeling both grounded and liberated, knowing that whatever the future holds, this moment had already become a cherished part of her journey.

Chapter 8

The morning light filtered softly through the sheer curtains, casting a warm, golden glow over the room. Outside, the early morning mist was just beginning to rise, wrapping the world in a hazy, dreamlike quality. The air was quiet, with only the faint sounds of birds stirring as dawn breaks. In this peaceful silence, Mira and Aatmaj lie entwined beneath the covers, both in a state of calm yet still brimming with the quiet, lingering energy of the night they shared.

Mira stirred, the weight of Aatmaj's arm around her waist grounding her, keeping her close in an embrace that felt as natural as breathing. The room smelled faintly of rain from the previous night and the subtle fragrance of jasmine drifting through the open window, blending with the warmth of their skin. She turned slightly, her gaze meeting his, and they shared a smile that held within it all the tenderness of their newfound connection.

In the quiet of the twilight, Aatmaj's hand moved gently along her back, his fingers tracing light patterns as though he's savouring each moment. There was an ease between them, a silent understanding that neither needed to rush nor to speak. He leaned forward, brushing his lips across her forehead, a touch so gentle it felt like a whisper. Mira closed her eyes, letting herself feel the sensation fully, warmth spreading from where his lips meet her skin.

As the morning light grew stronger, Mira felt a growing desire, a pull that brought her even closer to Aatmaj. She moved in closer, her fingers tracing along his collarbone, feeling the strength beneath his skin, her own heartbeat quickening. Their faces were close enough that their breaths intermingle, and Aatmaj's gaze moved from her eyes to her lips, a soft smile touching the corners of his mouth. Without needing words, they moved together, their bodies instinctively finding each other once more.

Their touches were slow, tender, every gesture filled with an unspoken affection that carried the intimacy of the night before. Aatmaj's hands found their way to Mira's sides, his fingers grazing the curves of her body, exploring with a careful reverence. Mira felt a shiver course through her, her own hands traveling along his chest, feeling blood running through his veins, muscles flexing beautifully.

In this quiet morning embrace, every touch felt amplified, every sensation heightened by the early light and the tranquillity of the world around them. They moved together, lost in each other, savouring the intimacy of the moment and the connection they had built. There was no urgency, only a deep sense of presence, as they let themselves be fully vulnerable, fully opened with each other.

When they finally parted, lying side by side, their fingers remained intertwined, and they exchanged a look that spoke of shared joy, understanding, and a sense of peace. The morning around them was quiet, serene, and in that moment, they both felt a deep contentment, knowing they had found something meaningful in each other.

Chapter 9

Mira found herself standing on unfamiliar terrain, a surreal, crimson landscape stretching endlessly around her. The ground beneath her feet was a dark, almost blood-red sand, warm to the touch, as if charged with a strange energy. The sky glowed in deep shades of orange and red, casting an ethereal light over everything. In the distance, an enormous sun hovered low on the horizon, so massive that it seemed to engulf the heavens. It was setting slowly, casting long, eerie shadows across towering, jagged mountains that loomed impossibly high, their peaks vanishing into thick, swirling clouds.

Ahead of her was an ocean unlike any she had seen—a vast, turbulent sea with waves as tall as buildings, crashing violently against each other in unpredictable patterns. The water was a dark, metallic blue with hints of purples and blacks, giving it an ominous, otherworldly sheen. It roared like a creature alive, each wave cresting and then breaking with a force that sent tremors through the ground beneath her.

Mira took a tentative step forward, feeling both awe and trepidation rise within her. She had entered this world almost as if through a dream, finding herself pulled by a strange force that compelled her to explore. Curiosity burned in her chest, but her instincts warned her of the dangers that lurked within these monstrous tides. As she continued walking from the shore toward the deeper waters, her heart pounded, every step a battle between her curiosity and her fear.

The air around her was thick and humid, carrying a strange scent, a mixture of salt and an unfamiliar, earthy fragrance. Her breath came in shallow gasps as she edged closer to the shoreline, her feet sinking slightly into the wet sand. The waves surged and receded, leaving patterns in the sand, as if telling stories of ancient creatures and lost civilizations. She felt a strange pull from the ocean, as though it was calling her name, beckoning her to come closer, to surrender to its depths.

Just then, Mira noticed movement in the distance, near the edge of the water. A figure emerged from the misty haze, walking toward her. It was a woman, draped in flowing, iridescent fabric that shimmered like the surface of the ocean itself, shifting in hues of blues and greens with every step she took. Her hair was silver and cascaded down her back, framing a face that seemed both ancient and youthful, her eyes glowing with an unnatural light.

As the woman approached, Mira felt a chill run through her, despite the heat of this strange world. The woman's presence was otherworldly, exuding a power and wisdom that felt almost divine. Yet, there was a sadness in her gaze, a depth of emotion that hinted at long-buried pain.

"Welcome, Mira," the woman said, her voice soft yet echoing like the waves themselves. "I have been waiting for you."

Mira's pulse quickened. She didn't know how this woman knew her name, but she felt an instinctive trust mixed with a sense of awe. "Where... where am I?" she asked, her voice barely a whisper.

The woman's gaze turned toward the massive sun setting behind the mountains, her expression contemplative. "You are in a realm between worlds, a place where memories, dreams, and ancient souls meet. Here, the ocean carries the stories of the past, and the sun sets on the edge of eternity. You have crossed into the Realm of Lost Reflections."

Mira shivered, feeling the weight of the woman's words. "Why am I here? How did I come to this place?"

The woman looked back at Mira, her gaze penetrating. "You were brought here by your own soul's yearning. You are a whisperer, Mira, a bridge between the realms. This place has called you because you are ready to see what has been hidden from you."

Mira swallowed, feeling a mix of anticipation and fear. The ocean roared louder as if responding to the woman's words, the waves crashing with a renewed intensity. She glanced toward the water, noticing shapes swirling beneath the surface—fleeting, shadowy forms that seemed to rise and sink back into the depths. They appeared almost like spirits, entities trapped within the ocean's embrace.

The woman extended a hand toward the waves, and as she did, the water calmed, its monstrous tides receding slightly, revealing a pathway that seemed to lead into the ocean itself. "There is much you must understand, but first, you must face what lies beneath. The ocean holds memories of pain, loss, and love— stories that have been forgotten, even by those who lived them."

Mira took a step closer to the woman, feeling an overwhelming urge to follow her, despite the fear gnawing at her heart. "Who… who are you?" she asked, her voice barely audible above the sound of the waves.

The woman smiled, a bittersweet expression that hinted at lifetimes of experience. "I am the Keeper of Reflections, a guide for those who, like you, are ready to confront the hidden parts of themselves. I am here to help you unlock what you have hidden, to understand the past lives and the shadows that have shaped you."

As the woman's words sank in, Mira felt a strange sense of recognition, as if she had known this woman across lifetimes. She felt an inexplicable pull toward the ocean, the waves now gentle and inviting, almost like an open door. The Keeper held out her hand, inviting Mara to walk with her toward the deeper waters.

With a deep breath, Mira took the Keeper's hand, stepping onto the path that stretched into the ocean. The water felt cool against her feet, soothing yet charged with energy. Each step brought her closer to something unknown, something she both feared and longed to face. The deeper they went, the more Mira felt as if she was shedding layers of herself, releasing burdens she had carried without realizing.

They walked in silence, the ocean calm around them, until they reached a point where the water reached Mira's waist. The

Keeper stopped, turning to Mira with a solemn expression. "What you seek lies beneath. Close your eyes, Mira, and let the water reveal to you the memories you have buried."

Mira hesitated, but the Keeper's steady gaze gave her the courage she needed. She closed her eyes, feeling the water rise around her, cool and heavy, as if drawing her into a trance. Images began to form in her mind—fragments of lives she hadn't known she'd lived, faces she'd loved and lost, pain and joy she'd felt across lifetimes.

The memories swirled around her like the currents, overwhelming yet strangely familiar. She saw herself as a healer in one life, a mother in another, a warrior in yet another—each life filled with its own lessons, its own struggles. Each memory seemed to leave a mark on her soul, shaping who she was and guiding her toward this moment.

As the visions faded, Mira opened her eyes, feeling tears streaming down her face. The Keeper looked at her with a gentle understanding, her own eyes reflecting the wisdom of countless lifetimes.

"You are a part of all that has come before," the Keeper said softly. "And you carry these stories within you. Remember them, Mira, and let them guide you as you walk your path."

Mira nodded, feeling a profound sense of peace settle over her. The ocean's tide began to recede, and the Keeper's form grew faint, her figure blending into the water until she was gone, leaving Mira alone with the memories that now pulsed within her.

As she made her way back to the shore, the sun dipped lower, casting its final rays across the ocean. Mira felt transformed, as if she had shed an old skin, emerging with a new understanding of herself and her purpose. She knew that her journey as a whisperer was just beginning and that the ocean of memories would always be there, guiding her whenever she needed to remember the deeper truths of her soul.

As Mira stood on the shore of that mysterious realm, watching the Keeper's form fade into the waves, a wave of recognition washed over her. That woman, that otherworldly guide who had shown her the ocean of memories and her own forgotten lives— she wasn't just a stranger from this spectral realm. She was someone from Mira's own life on Earth. She was Nani, her grandmother: a soul of kindness, wisdom, and warmth, whose lessons had shaped Mira's heart and spirit in ways she hadn't fully understood until now. Forms could be different but essence of them is the real deal. This realization made Mira's heart swell with love and gratitude.

Mira's mind was flooded with memories, vivid as if they'd just happened. Her Nani was a small woman with a gentle, weathered face, her eyes forever kind yet filled with a mysterious depth, as if she could see through people, right down to their souls. Her skin was soft and creased with the delicate lines of laughter and care, and her hands, though roughened from years of working with plants and herbs, always moved with a soothing, healing touch. Her dark hair, streaked with silver, was always braided or wrapped in a scarf, her attire simple—usually a cotton saree in earthy colours, rich greens or soft browns, the kind that made her look as though she'd grown out of the earth herself.

Mira remembered summers spent in her Nani's garden, which seemed like an enchanted forest, hidden away in a small corner of her family's land. The garden was wild and lush, with herbs, flowering plants, and trees arching overhead, casting dappled sunlight onto the paths below. Nani taught her how to recognize plants by their shapes, their smells, their textures. To Mira, each leaf, each stem, seemed to have its own story, and Nani knew every one of them by heart. She spoke to the plants as if they were old friends, and in her presence, Mira found herself doing the same.

"Plants are healers, Mira," Nani would say, her voice soft and reverent. "They give us life, food, medicine. They're always listening, always ready to help. But you have to respect them. You must give them your trust, and they will give you their magic."

Under Nani's guidance, Mira learned how to prepare simple herbal remedies. She remembered watching Nani crush leaves and roots, blending them into pastes or boiling them into tonics, each mixture a work of devotion. There were tonics for fever, balms for cuts, teas to ease troubled minds. And though young Mira hadn't fully understood, she sensed that Nani's hands held a rare gift, a gift that seemed to live in her very bones. Over time, Mira would feel that same gift awakening within her, like a seed taking root.

But Nani's gifts went beyond herbs and healing. She was a storyteller, and her tales were as rich as the earth itself. In the evenings, after the cooking was done, they would sit together on the veranda, the air scented with the night-blooming jasmine from the garden. Nani would tell Mira stories of their ancestors—people who had lived simple lives but held profound wisdom, people who, like Nani, had been healers, dreamers, guides. She'd tell stories of mystical places where spirits walked freely, of dreams that held messages, of signs and symbols from the universe. These weren't fairy tales; they were lessons wrapped in ancient lore, passed down from generation to generation.

One story in particular had always lingered in Mira's memory. Nani had spoken of a woman in their lineage, long ago, who had been known as a whisperer. She could listen to the voices of spirits and understand the hidden messages of the stars. She was revered, not feared, because she used her gifts to help, to heal, and to guide others on their paths. "It's in our blood, Mira," Nani had whispered, her eyes twinkling with a secret knowledge. "One day, you'll understand. It's a rare thing to carry such gifts. But it comes with a responsibility, to serve and to honour the life you're given."

It was with Nani that Mira had learned the joys of cooking, too, though Nani's approach was less about recipes and more about feeling. She would never measure ingredients, simply taking handfuls of spices, leaves, or grains, her hands moving instinctively, her sense of flavour and aroma her only guide. Together, they would cook fragrant dals and spicy curries, dishes infused with love and warmth. And when Mira stirred the pots or ground the spices, Nani would smile approvingly, telling her to listen, to feel the energy of each ingredient, as if cooking were a way to connect with the spirit of nature itself.

Nani's presence was a force of comfort and strength in Mira's life, an anchor. But as Mira grew older, she noticed a sadness in her grandmother's eyes, a far-off look that hinted at something she couldn't share. Nani would sometimes wander into the garden at dusk and sit quietly among the plants, as if communing with spirits only she could see.

Then, one winter evening, Nani was gone. Her passing was sudden, almost mysterious, like the ending of one of her own tales. There were whispers among the family that she had simply faded, her soul crossing into another realm as gently as a leaf falling from a tree. Her mysterious departure left a void in Mira's heart, a wound that only deepened when she realized how much she had yet to learn from her. But Nani's presence lingered in every herb Mira picked, every story she told, every healing touch she offered.

In the years after Nani's passing, Mira began to notice signs of her grandmother's gifts emerging in herself. She would have vivid dreams, sometimes of Nani herself, standing in the garden, smiling, or whispering words that Mira could only half-hear. She found herself drawn to the art of healing, not just with plants but with her voice, her presence, her intuition. And when she finally began her journey as a whisperer, Nani's words, stories, and wisdom felt like guides, lighting her path.

Now, as she stood in the otherworldly realm, Mira realized that Nani's spirit had always been with her, not just as a memory but as a living presence, a guide in the quiet spaces of her heart. Her grandmother had passed on to her not only the knowledge of herbs and stories but a sense of purpose, a duty to serve, to heal, to understand the hidden realms of life.

Mira closed her eyes, breathing deeply, feeling Nani's presence as if she were right beside her. She could almost hear her grandmother's voice, warm and wise: "The world is more than you see, Mira. Remember, there is beauty in the unknown, and power in the unseen. Trust yourself. Trust the gifts you've been given. They are yours for a reason."

Mira opened her eyes, filled with a newfound sense of peace, strength, and gratitude. She knew her journey was just beginning, but she also knew she was not alone. Nani was with her, in every breath, in every heartbeat, in every step forward. And as she looked out at the waves of this strange realm, she felt ready to face whatever came next, knowing she carried within her the legacy of love, wisdom, and healing that her grandmother had so selflessly passed on.

She never lost her dear Nani ever. This thought itself was so powerful that Mira started smiling thinking about this new found reality. Reality which is not a feeling or hunch but profound and concrete.

Chapter 10

The market was bustling with life as Mira stepped into the familiar scene, the smells and sounds swirling around her like an embrace. It was the heart of the late afternoon, when the sun cast long shadows, and the colours of the vegetables and fruits seemed to pop with an almost surreal intensity. Baskets overflowed with vibrant greens, fiery reds, and sunny yellows, a palette of nature's finest offerings spread out under the open sky. There were stacks of plump tomatoes, leafy greens as crisp as morning dew, fiery red chilies, and rows of carrots so bright they looked as if they'd been painted in shades of orange.

Mira navigated her way through the crowd, smiling at a few familiar faces. The vendors called out, each vying for attention, their voices a blend of friendly banter and earnest persuasion. The air was filled with the scents of fresh coriander, earthy potatoes, and pungent ginger. She reached the vegetable stall run by Vinod, a lively man with a smile that reached his eyes, who always had a witty comment or two ready for Mira.

"Ah, Mira Madam!" Vinod greeted her, beaming. "Back again, and just in time! I kept the freshest spinach aside for you—I knew you'd come looking."

Mira laughed, shaking her head. "Vinod, you always say that. But I'm sure you keep the 'freshest' spinach for every customer."

"Oh no, not every customer," he said, holding up his hand as if making a solemn vow. "Only my most discerning ones—the ones who can tell their methi from their palak without even touching it!"

Mira rolled her eyes, amused. She picked up a bunch of spinach, inspecting its dark, crisp leaves, then moved on to examine a stack of tomatoes. She pressed each one gently, looking for just the right level of ripeness. "I need the best for tomorrow. I'm hosting a dinner party, and my guests have high standards," she said, casting Vinod a playful, conspiratorial look.

"Ah, yes, I see!" Vinod smirked, winking at her. "Then I shall make sure they don't question your culinary expertise. Only the finest for you!" He picked up a particularly plump tomato, holding it up as if presenting a rare gem. "Look at this beauty! This tomato has the charm of a Bollywood star and the freshness of the morning breeze. Perfect for a party."

Mira laughed, tossing it into her basket. "If only it could cook itself into a delicious curry as well!"

He chuckled, arranging the vegetables around him with a flourish. "Now that, madam, would be magic. But I leave the magic to you."

She added a bunch of fresh coriander, bright and fragrant, into her basket. Next, she turned to the eggplants, trying to pick the ones that felt the firmest and had a glossy sheen. Vinod, ever observant, leaned in. "Ah, planning on making baingan bharta, are we?" She raised her eyebrows. "How did you guess?"

"Oh, madam, I've seen you eyeing the eggplants like that before," he said, shrugging with a grin. "I know your game." Mira couldn't help but laugh. "You know too much, Vinod!

Fine, yes. I am making bharta. And some aloo-gobi, too. So, make sure these cauliflowers are as good as they look."

Vinod handed her a plump cauliflower, dusting it off like a prized possession. "This one's as fresh as the Himalayas, madam. And just for you, I'll even give you a discount!" "Oh, don't flatter yourself," she teased. "You always say that, then sneak in a little extra on the weight."

"Ah, madam, I have to make a living somehow!" he laughed, handing her a paper bag filled with potatoes. "But for you, I'll even throw in a bit of ginger and garlic. Party essentials, no?" She nodded, feeling her bag grow heavy with the weight of her selections. "Absolutely. Now just some lemons, and I think I'm set."

Vinod handed her a handful of bright yellow lemons, fragrant with their sharp, fresh scent. He counted out her total, and she handed him a few crisp bills. Just as she turned to leave, Vinod leaned in with a smirk. "Madam, with these vegetables, your party is guaranteed to be a hit. And if anyone asks where you got them, just say it's Vinod's secret stash."

Mira laughed, waving as she made her way back into the bustling crowd, her heart light with the joy of her little market adventure. As she walked home, she could already envision her kitchen filled with the smell of garlic frying, cumin seeds spluttering in oil, and the delightful sizzle of vegetables cooking. It was these simple, vibrant moments that brought her true contentment—an evening of laughter, a dinner table filled with colour and warmth, all brought together by a trip to the lively market and the kindness of people like Vinod, whose humour and care had left her with a smile to last the evening.

Chapter 11

Mira's circle of friends was unlike any other. They called themselves "The Seekers," a small, spirited group bound not just by the memories of that fateful Himalayan trek but by a shared thirst for exploring the mysteries of life, the hidden realms, and the depths of the human soul. They'd met on that journey as strangers, brought together by the snow-laden landscapes, the thin, bracing air, and the primal sense of awe that only the towering peaks of the Himalayas could inspire. Each of them had come for their own reasons, but something about the experience had woven their souls together. From then on, they were each other's chosen family—a family that met once every three months to dive deep into the mysteries of existence.

As Mira prepared for their gathering, memories of that first trek washed over her—starlit nights beside a campfire, ancient villages perched on cliffs, their simple beauty and tranquillity. It was there, amidst snow-covered peaks, that she'd discovered her own untapped potential, with these new friends as her guides. They were a unique bunch, each one steeped in a different branch of occult wisdom, and over the years, they'd shared their practices with Mira, helping her shape her path as a time whisperer and healer.

Ranjan – The Astrologer and Numerologist

Ranjan was a man of numbers and stars, a corporate strategist by profession, but a seeker of cosmic knowledge by calling. He had a calm, grounded presence, with eyes that seemed to hold galaxies within them. He wore simple clothes, always preferring muted colours, and carried a notebook filled with mysterious numbers, charts, and astrological symbols wherever he went. Ranjan was deeply committed to astrology and numerology, seeing them as a bridge between fate and free will. He believed that by understanding the stars' positions and the vibrations of numbers, one could glimpse the blueprint of a person's destiny.

Through Ranjan, Mira learned to read astrological charts, understand planetary influences, and appreciate the subtle power of numbers. He would often remind her, "Mira, the stars don't dictate—only illuminate. Free will is always yours." His insights helped her recognize patterns and cycles not just in her own life, but in those she guided, enriching her work as a healer.

Meeta – The Crystal Healer and Energy Worker

Meeta was a radiant presence, always adorned with crystals and gemstones that sparkled like tiny prisms, catching the light wherever she went. She had an unshakeable belief in the energies of the Earth and was deeply attuned to the vibrations of stones and minerals. A gentle soul, Meeta worked as an environmental scientist, spending her days protecting the land she loved, and her nights studying the energies of the Earth's gifts. Her home was a treasure trove of crystals, and she treated each stone with reverence, seeing them as allies in the healing process.

Meeta introduced Mira to the world of crystal healing, teaching her how to use various stones to cleanse spaces, balance energy, and strengthen intuition. With Meeta's guidance, Mira learned the art of chakra alignment through crystals and the ways in which these ancient minerals could amplify intentions. Mira became captivated by this practice, learning to channel energies through stones to bring peace and balance to those who sought her healing.

Abhay – The Past-Life Regression Expert

Abhay, a former psychologist turned past-life regression therapist, was the most intense of the group. With his piercing gaze and quiet demeanour, he had a presence that seemed to see right through to a person's soul. Abhay was deeply passionate about his work, convinced that many of life's present difficulties stemmed from unresolved events in past lives. He had a vast knowledge of the subconscious mind and had spent years mastering the art of regression therapy, helping his clients confront past traumas and release old karmic bonds.

From Abhay, Mira learned the intricate techniques of guiding someone into a meditative state and uncovering the hidden memories buried within. His teachings resonated deeply with her own work as a time whisperer, and his influence helped her refine her approach to regression, teaching her how to guide her clients through the shadows of their own pasts with compassion and care. "Mira, the past isn't a prison," he'd once told her, "It's a lesson."

Ragini – The Tarot Reader and Divination Specialist

Ragini, with her vibrant scarves and always-painted nails, was the life of the group. An artist by profession, she worked as an illustrator but was drawn to the intuitive arts of tarot and other forms of divination. Her deck of cards, always within reach, seemed an extension of herself, and she treated each reading as a blend of art and magic. Ragini had an effervescent charm, always quick with a smile or a witty remark, but she took her tarot practice seriously, believing the cards to be a mirror reflecting the soul's innermost truths.

Ragini's playful, insightful readings taught Mira to embrace the intuitive side of her work. "The cards never lie," Ragini would say with a wink, "but they don't always tell you what you want to hear." Ragini taught Mira how to interpret subtle symbols, how to weave together intuition and imagery, and how to let the cards reveal the patterns and possibilities within each person's story.

Saraswati – The Herbalist and Wiccan

Saraswati, the oldest of the group, had a wisdom that was both deep and earthy. She was a retired botanist, her fingers always slightly stained from working with plants, her hair streaked with silver. Saraswati's home was filled with drying herbs and the aroma of concoctions simmering in pots, and her knowledge of plants was rivalled only by her reverence for nature's cycles. As a practicing Wiccan, she celebrated the Earth's rhythms, observing the solstices, equinoxes, and moon phases as part of her spiritual practice.

From Saraswati, Mira learned to create herbal remedies and potions, using plants not just for their physical healing properties but as spiritual allies. Saraswati taught her the importance of honouring each season and connecting with the elements. "Nature's magic is subtle," she would say, "but powerful." Under Saraswati's guidance, Mira developed her own herbal rituals, incorporating them into her healing practices.

Mira had found her soul's home among these friends, each one a guide in their own way. They met every three months, usually in one of their homes, though sometimes they'd choose a quiet forest clearing or a secluded beach, places where they could connect with nature and dive deep into their rituals. During their gatherings, they would share stories, exchange techniques, and practice together. Sometimes it was a meditation, other times a ritual or divination session. Each gathering was a blend of laughter, insight, and profound connection, an opportunity to learn and to lean on each other as they journeyed through life's mysteries.

The group valued Mira's kindness, her openness, and her intuitive gifts. Her curiosity and humility made her a joy to teach, and her abilities as a healer and time whisperer brought new dimensions to their gatherings. Mira's gift for empathy drew them to her, and they all sensed in her the same questing spirit that had brought them together in the first place.

Over time, Mira became an integral part of The Seekers, her presence as grounding as Ranjan's wisdom, as vibrant as Ragini's charm, as soothing as Meeta's crystals, as intense as Abhay's insights, and as wise as Saraswati's herbal lore. Their gatherings left Mira feeling renewed, each one a reminder that there was always more to learn, always another layer of existence waiting to be explored.

In those sacred moments with her friends, Mira felt truly alive, truly herself—a seeker among seekers, an adventurer in realms seen and unseen. And as they left each gathering, they carried forward the bond they had forged, a bond woven of shared dreams, mutual respect, and the enduring magic of friendship.

Chapter 12

Mira had been considering inviting Atmaj to her upcoming gathering with, The Seekers, for a while now. She thought back to their last few months together, the ways their conversations had deepened, the quiet understanding they shared that felt like a steady, pulsing energy between them. Atmaj had a natural curiosity and an open mind—traits Mira admired. Yet, despite their closeness, she hesitated.

There were a few reasons for her reservations. First, she worried about how Atmaj would fit into the group dynamic. The Seekers were more than just friends; they were a small, close-knit community, bound by shared secrets and a mutual respect for each other's practices. She wasn't sure if Atmaj, who wasn't deeply involved in the occult, would find himself at ease among them, especially with the more intense rituals or discussions of spiritual experiences that often surfaced during their gatherings.

Second, Mira knew The Seekers had their own ways of welcoming new members. They didn't mind introducing fresh faces now and then, but only if they sensed that the person was a seeker at heart, someone genuinely invested in exploring the realms beyond the ordinary. Atmaj was open-minded, yes, but Mira worried that he might feel like an outsider, someone who had walked into a private world that wasn't meant for him.

Lastly, she was concerned about their relationship. Inviting Atmaj into this intimate aspect of her life meant sharing a part of herself that she hadn't fully revealed to him. It was one thing to talk about her practices, to tell him about her work as a time whisperer, healer, and past-life regression therapist. It was another thing to let him witness it all firsthand, to see her interact with friends who had helped shape her spiritual journey. She wondered if letting him in like this would change the way he saw her—if he'd see her differently, or if it might create some kind of shift between them.

But as she thought more about it, she realized she was letting fear hold her back. Atmaj had never been one to judge or misunderstand; if anything, he had always supported her, respected her, and encouraged her growth. Mira smiled to herself, realizing she wanted him there. Perhaps The Seekers would find his unique insights refreshing, and perhaps, just perhaps, he might find something in their circle that resonated with him as well.

She decided to call him. She picked up her phone, dialling his number, and listened to the faint ring until he picked up. His familiar voice greeted her warmly.

"Atmaj, hey! Are you free to talk?" Mira asked, a hint of mischief in her tone.

"Of course, Mira. What's on your mind?" His voice was cheerful, as always, with a warmth that made her feel instantly at ease.

"Well, I have a bit of a proposition for you." She paused for effect, letting the curiosity build. "It's an invitation. But it comes with… conditions."

Atmaj laughed. "Conditions? This sounds serious. Tell me more."

Mira took a deep breath, choosing her words carefully. "Do you remember the friends I told you about, the ones I met during that trek in the Himalayas? We're meeting tomorrow evening, and… I'd like you to join us."

There was a slight pause on his end, then he responded with a smile in his voice. "I'd love to meet your friends, Mira. But, from the way you're building this up, it sounds like there's a catch."

"Well, sort of," she admitted, laughing. "This isn't exactly your average dinner party. They're a special group—very connected to the mystical, to different types of spiritual practices. Each of them is involved in something unique, like astrology, crystal healing, and regression therapy. We gather, share experiences, perform small rituals, meditate together. It's… a world I'm not sure you're fully prepared for." She softened her voice, adding, "But I want you to be a part of it if you'd like to."

He took it in, his silence a thoughtful one. Then, with his usual playful edge, he asked, "Will there be chanting and dancing under the moon?"

"Possibly," she teased back, her laughter ringing out. "But seriously, it's a bit more than that. I just want you to be open-minded. They're all lovely, each a little quirky, maybe intense, but genuine souls. They've taught me a lot, and… they know me as deeply as anyone does."

Atmaj's voice softened, sincerity lacing his words. "Mira, I'd be honoured to meet them. And don't worry—I'll do my best to keep up with the quirks and mysteries. After all, I know the quirkiest one of all," he added with a chuckle.

"Oh, ha-ha," Mira said, rolling her eyes, though she couldn't help but smile. "Well, I'll warn them about your charm and your endless sarcasm."

"Perfect, prepare them for the worst. But honestly, Mira, I'm touched you'd invite me. I'll keep my heart and mind wide open. Promise."

Mira felt a warmth spread through her chest. "Thank you, Atmaj. I can't wait to introduce you to them. Maybe you'll see a new side of me, too."

"Then I'm in for a double treat," he replied, his voice low and full of affection. "What should I bring?"

"Just yourself. And maybe a spirit of adventure." She paused, a smile lighting up her face. "I'm ready, Mira," he said, his voice warm and steady. "Can't wait to explore this world with you."

Chapter 13

The dinner table was alive with laughter, stories, and the comforting clink of cutlery against plates. The scent of herbs, spices, and freshly baked flatbreads filled the air, mingling with the warmth of familiar voices and the joy of good company. Mira looked around, feeling the deep satisfaction of having her friends together, with Atmaj beside her as part of the group.

They sat around an old, polished wooden table, under the soft glow of candles. Outside, a gentle breeze rustled through the trees, and the faint sound of crickets created a soothing backdrop to their voices. Plates piled high with vibrant vegetables, steaming bowls of soup, and fragrant rice made the table an inviting spread, each dish a reflection of Mira's love for nourishing food.

Ranjan – The Cosmic Story

Ranjan, with his usual thoughtful expression and twinkling eyes, was the first to speak. He had been talking to Atmaj about his work, explaining the significance of the stars and numbers in guiding one's life.

"You know," Ranjan said, placing his fork down as he warmed up to his story, "I once had a client who was on the verge of leaving his family business. He'd always felt it was his father's path, not his own, and he was ready to walk away." Ranjan paused, looking around the table. "But when I ran his astrological chart, I saw a strong alignment between the planets and the houses of family tind wealth. It was as if the universe had woven him into that role, not as a cage, but as a source of strength."

Ranjan leaned forward, his voice low and rich with mystery. "I suggested he stay with the business, not just for duty but as a path to fulfil his own potential. He listened, hesitantly at first, but within a year, he was able to innovate and expand the business in ways his father hadn't imagined. He later told me it was like tapping into an ancient energy that had always been his to wield."

The group nodded, caught up in Ranjan's tale. Mira saw the spark of curiosity in Atmaj's eyes, knowing he was fascinated by the unseen forces that guided lives.

Meeta – The Crystal Encounter

After a moment of quiet, Meeta spoke up, her voice soft but animated as she adjusted the crystal pendant around her neck. "I've had a few encounters where crystals seemed to find me, rather than the other way around," she said with a knowing smile. "One time, I was visiting a small village in Rajasthan and came across an old man selling rough stones on a mat. Among all the brown and black rocks, there was one deep purple amethyst, glowing under the sun as if it were alive."

She glanced at Mira, her friend in both spirit and practice. "The man didn't know the stone's value, so I offered him a fair price, and he smiled at me in this strange, almost knowing way. When I got home, I meditated with the amethyst, and suddenly, I felt this rush of calm, a feeling like it was guiding me. It taught me how to use amethyst to heal emotional wounds in my clients. Since then, that crystal has been my talisman—it's like a companion."

Meeta's words hung in the air, a reminder of the quiet wisdom she carried. Everyone nodded, moved by the gentle yet powerful story.

Abhay – The Forgotten Past

Abhay, with his intense gaze and contemplative aura, picked up from there. "Crystals are lovely, but I've always found my calling in the subconscious mind," he said, his voice as calm and steady as a deep river. "Last year, I had a client who couldn't shake this sense of dread. It was affecting his health, his relationships, everything. Through regression therapy, we discovered he'd lived as a warrior in a past life—one who had betrayed his own kin."

Abhay's eyes held the intensity of his own journey with past lives as he shared this. "The guilt he felt had lingered across lifetimes, becoming this dark cloud over his soul. But once we brought it to light, he was able to forgive himself, to release that ancient guilt."

Mira, who had also dabbled in regression therapy under Abhay's guidance, felt a deep sense of gratitude for his work. She saw how Atmaj listened, riveted, perhaps for the first time considering how echoes of the past could shape the present.

Ragini – The Cards that Don't Lie

Ragini, ever playful, tilted her head and jumped in. "Well, my experiences are less intense, but still spooky," she said, her fingers playing with a ring on her hand. "Last month, I did a tarot reading for a woman who asked me if she should leave her job. Now, you know I don't sugarcoat readings." She grinned mischievously. "The cards showed me the Tower and the Chariot—destruction and movement. Not exactly what she wanted to hear, right?"

Ragini leaned in, her voice taking on a mischievous edge. "I told her change was coming, like it or not. She was sceptical, but within two weeks, her company announced layoffs. She ended up getting an offer for a new job that gave her more freedom than she'd ever had." She threw her hands up with a laugh. "The cards may not always be gentle, but they're honest."

Her story left the table chuckling, especially Atmaj, who seemed fascinated by the cards' ability to speak so plainly yet so mysteriously.

Saraswati – The Gift of Herbs

Saraswati, with her gentle wisdom, was the last to share. She held her tea in her hands, the light from the candles reflecting in her kind eyes. "I'll share a story from many years ago," she began. "I was in the mountains studying plants, and an elderly woman, a healer from a nearby village, took me under her wing. She showed me how to gather herbs with intention, to honour each plant before picking it. 'Every plant has a spirit,' she'd tell me. 'Treat it with respect, and it will lend you its power.'"

Her gaze grew distant, as if she were seeing that wise healer again. "She taught me how to make tinctures, poultices, and potions—not just for the body, but for the soul. I remember watching her heal a young man with nothing but crushed mint leaves and a prayer. He was burning with fever, and I thought nothing could save him, but she whispered to the leaves, applied them, and he recovered by morning."

The group was silent for a moment, soaking in her tale. Atmaj was clearly taken with her story, his respect for this kind of wisdom evident in the way he listened.

Mira's Turn to Speak

Finally, the attention turned to Mira. She felt the warmth of her friends' eyes on her, each one a reminder of the gifts they'd shared with her over the years. Atmaj looked at her with quiet curiosity, as if he were seeing a new side of her in the presence of these old friends.

"Well," Mira began, her smile soft, "I guess you could say each of you has been a teacher to me. Ranjan taught me that life's rhythms are written in the stars, Meeta showed me the language of stones, Abhay opened the doors of the past, Ragini taught me to see through the cards, and Saraswati showed me that plants are not just remedies but allies."

She reached for Atmaj's hand, a gentle connection that went unnoticed by the others but meant everything to her. "Each of you has shaped my journey, helping me become the healer and the time whisperer I am today. And Atmaj," she added, her voice soft, "has brought his own energy into my life—a spark, a reminder to stay grounded and to live fully in the present."

The group looked at Mira and Atmaj, seeing the warmth between them, a light that spoke of new beginnings. Laughter and conversation continued, each story another reminder of the mysteries they shared, the wisdom they brought into each other's lives. Atmaj, embraced by this circle of seekers, felt himself becoming a part of this world, one story, one laugh, and one shared moment at a time.

Under the velvet canopy of a starlit night, Mira and her friends gathered on the terrace, laughing and talking, their spirits lifted by the warmth of friendship and the satisfaction of a hearty dinner. The air was crisp, the quiet hum of the night punctuated by occasional bursts of laughter.

The stars above seemed unusually bright, as if they were winking down on the group, lending their silent rhythm to the moment. Mira looked around at her friends, each face lit by a soft, otherworldly glow that seemed to unite them all in that one magical instant. Without speaking, Mira stretched out her hand to Meeta, who grinned knowingly and took it. One by one, the others followed, joining hands until they formed a complete circle, a closed circuit of energy, vibrating with anticipation.

Atmaj leaned against the terrace railing, his eyes glinting with curiosity and quiet admiration. He had known Mira long enough to understand that something profound was about to unfold. Still, he couldn't shake the awe he felt each time Mira led them into one of her mystical, spontaneous adventures.

As the circle tightened, Mira's voice broke the silence. "Feel the stars," she whispered, closing her eyes and taking a deep breath. "Let them guide you. They've been here long before us, and they'll be here long after."

A faint hum began to rise from the group, an unspoken melody that each person seemed to sense in their bones. There was no music, but in that silence, a rhythm pulsed, an invisible beat that linked their heartbeats and steps.

One of the friends, Ranjan, opened his eyes and whispered, "It's like... we're moving to the music of the universe."

"Shh," Mira smiled, her eyes twinkling with a mix of mystery and delight. "Don't speak, just listen."

They began to sway, each body moving in perfect harmony, their movements a language only they seemed to understand. Arms lifted, hands stretched toward the heavens as if trying to touch the stars themselves. The group turned and spun, each step synchronized, as if rehearsed for years, though no one had ever planned this dance.

Atmaj's mouth fell slightly open as he watched. The scene before him seemed surreal, as if he were witnessing a timeless ritual, a dance older than history itself. He felt something stir inside him, a sensation both familiar and foreign, a call he couldn't quite understand.

Ragini, spinning near Mira, laughed softly. "This is insane," she said under her breath, but her feet kept moving, her body entirely in sync with the group.

Mira's smile widened, and she tilted her head towards Atmaj, calling out, "Join us, Atmaj! Feel the energy!"

Atmaj shook his head, laughing nervously. "No, no. I think I'll mess up your perfect rhythm."

"Oh, come on!" Mira coaxed, holding out a hand. "There's no such thing as messing up here. We're just... being."

With a hesitant smile, Atmaj took a deep breath and stepped forward, reaching for Mira's hand. The moment he joined the circle, he felt a surge of warmth and energy coursing through him, as if he'd plugged into an unseen current. The invisible beat caught him, and before he knew it, he was moving with the same flow, his body swaying to a rhythm he couldn't hear but could feel in every fibre of his being.

"See?" Mira whispered, her eyes sparkling as she caught his gaze. "You're part of it too."

The dance continued, fluid and seamless, as they twirled under the vastness of the night sky. No one spoke, yet everyone understood. It was as though their spirits had merged into one, moving with a single heartbeat. The silence of the terrace filled with the sound of their synchronized breaths, their feet grazing the floor in perfect harmony.

Time seemed to stretch and dissolve, the moment expanding into something infinite. Mira closed her eyes, losing herself in the dance, feeling each star above them as if it were breathing along with them, guiding their steps. She felt Atmaj's presence nearby, his energy blending with the others, adding a new, curious note to the symphony they had created.

After what felt like eternity, the group slowed, their movements softening, until finally, they came to a standstill, their breaths mingling in the cool night air. They opened their eyes, smiling at each other with a newfound depth of connection, a silent understanding that transcended words.

Atmaj was the first to break the silence, still slightly breathless. "That... that was incredible," he said, looking at each of them in amazement. "I don't know what just happened, but... thank you."

Mira placed a gentle hand on his shoulder, her eyes filled with warmth and wisdom. "Sometimes, the best moments aren't planned. They just... happen when we let go."

Saraswati chimed in, her voice soft and full of wonder, "I felt like I was part of something much bigger than myself. Like... we were tapping into the pulse of the universe."

Meeta nodded, her eyes misty with emotion. "It was like... the stars were dancing with us."

They stood there in silence for a moment longer, each lost in their thoughts, savouring the memory of their cosmic dance. The terrace felt different now, as if it held a fragment of the magic they had shared, a piece of that invisible music lingering in the air.

Mira took a deep breath, gazing up at the stars. "Tonight was special," she murmured, almost to herself. "A reminder that we're never really alone, that there's always something bigger guiding us, watching over us."

The others followed her gaze, their eyes reflecting the starlight. In that instant, they felt a connection not only with each other but with the vastness of the universe, a bond that transcended time and space.

Atmaj looked at Mira, his admiration clear in his eyes. "You have this way of making ordinary moments feel... extraordinary. Thank you, Mira."

Mira smiled, a soft, knowing smile. "The magic is in all of us. Sometimes, we just need a reminder."

The group lingered on the terrace, basking in the quiet aftermath of their dance, their hearts full, their spirits lifted. The stars above twinkled brighter than ever, as if sharing in the joy of their shared moment, a silent witness to the bond that now tied them together forever.

Chapter 14

The evening settled into a hushed silence, Atmaj and Mira found themselves alone in the warmth of his home, satisfied by the joyous gathering. Together, they quietly tidied up, sharing smiles and unspoken conversations, savouring the lingering traces of laughter and conversations that filled the night.

Finally, with the house immaculate and calm, they climbed the stairs to the terrace. Under the vast, starlit sky, they laid down their bedding—a soft, warm place beneath a gentle blanket of night. The sky stretched endlessly above, its stars like silent witnesses to their quiet contentment. The cool night air brushed against them, carrying the faint scents of earth and jasmine, blending into a delicate, soothing fragrance that filled their senses.

Mira, lying next to Atmaj, let her mind drift as she gazed at the stars, feeling a deep sense of connection to something greater. In this tranquil space, she began to hum, her voice effortlessly sliding into the hauntingly beautiful Raag Shivranjani. Her voice took shape, wrapping around the melody of "Re sajana, tum bin kalna, na hi pare mann tann rang chaina," her notes flowing like a gentle river, weaving into the night.

Atmaj lay spellbound beside her, his body attuned to every note, every vibration. Her voice washed over him, and he felt himself unravel, dissolving into the music. Every cell in his being resonated with Mira's song, blending into the same rhythm. The boundaries between his body and the sound began to dissolve, as though each note was a thread pulling him into a dimension beyond thought, beyond form—a place of pure sensation, peace, and oneness.

In that moment, Atmaj felt transported, lifted from the physical world into a realm of pure emotion and energy, where the stars seemed to pulse with every phrase she sang. He felt as though he was floating within the vast night, a tiny spark of life cradled within the universe's embrace, yet intricately bound to Mira's voice, which guided him gently through this otherworldly landscape.

As the final notes of Mira's song faded into silence, Atmaj felt a deep, blissful calm wash over him. With soft, drowsy smiles, they nestled into the warmth beside each other, letting the world drift away. Enveloped by the night's serenity and each other's presence, they slipped into a deep, peaceful sleep under the watchful gaze of the stars, like two souls content in their shared rhythm.

Chapter 15

A few days after their magical night on the terrace, Mira received an unexpected invitation from an acquaintance—a friend of a friend. The invitation beckoned her to a sacred ritual near the mountains of the Western Ghats in southern India, a region Mira knew well, having journeyed there before. She shared the news with Atmaj, and without a second thought, they decided to go, sensing the mystery and excitement that awaited them.

Their journey began with a train winding its way southward, the landscape changing from cityscapes to lush, dense forests as the mountains loomed closer. On arrival, they rented a car, which rumbled through narrow mountain paths, the air growing thick with the scent of wet earth and rich vegetation. The trees grew dense, almost guarding the path ahead, as if hiding the secrets of the place they were heading to. Their destination was secretive and sacred, known to few, tucked away from the prying eyes of the world. When they reached a clearing at the heart of the forest, they saw a gathering of twenty or so people, a mix of men and women who stood silently around a crackling fire.

In the centre, a head priestess, draped in earthy fabrics, stood before the fire, her voice a low murmur as she chanted ancient mantras. The words were soft, barely audible, but Mira could feel their power weaving through the air, creating an invisible tapestry that bound them all together. The energy around the fire intensified, a heady blend of the sacred and the primal. A drumbeat started, steady and hypnotic, pulsing like the heartbeat of the earth itself.

Each person was free to let the rhythm guide them in whatever way they wished. Some closed their eyes, slipping into deep meditation; others moved with the beat, letting their bodies sway and dance with abandon. Laughter and cries of joy filled the air as some surrendered to pure ecstasy, while others observed, absorbing the scene with quiet reverence. Mira and Atmaj felt the drumbeats throb within, drawing them into the mystical rhythm. The ritual wove on for hours, each moment drawing them deeper into its trance.

As the ritual gradually came to an end, people began drifting back to the ordinary world, bidding farewell with heartfelt hugs and lingering smiles. Mira and Atmaj lingered, enchanted by the beauty of the moment. The forest around them felt alive, its shadows pulsing with the energy left by the gathering.

A few others stayed, sharing quiet conversations under the moonlight. Mira and Atmaj held each other, laughing and embracing as if intoxicated by the raw freedom of the night. They felt an uncontainable joy surge within them, and they broke into a spontaneous run, laughing as they darted through the trees like children in a game of hide and seek. Then, suddenly, Mira stopped.

She stood still, gazing into the forest depths as if called by something unseen. Her expression turned trance-like, her breath slowing as if she were listening to a secret melody. One by one, she began to slip out of her clothes, her movements calm and entranced. Atmaj watched, captivated, feeling drawn into the same spell that seemed to have overtaken her. Silently, he followed as Mira continued deeper into the forest, stepping lightly over roots and rocks, until they reached a massive, flat stone in a small clearing, illuminated by a thin shaft of moonlight.

Without a word, her gaze unwavering as she looked up at Atmaj. Her eyes held a fierce, piercing intensity, as if seeing him from another world. The silence between them was charged, timeless, and in that sacred space, they understood each other completely. The energy of the ritual, the mystery of the forest, and the beauty of the moment melded together as Atmaj moved closer, their souls entwined as they surrendered to the ancient magic of the night.

Chapter 16

In the heart of the jungle, where the sun's rays started filtering through the dense canopy above, dappling the earth with golden light, she lay nestled on a stone bed, a natural formation smoothed by the passage of time. The air was thick with the scent of earth and blooming flora, remnants of last night's vibrant dance still swirling in her veins. Her body, kissed by the warmth of the morning, was a canvas painted with the hues of the night's revelries—soft whispers of laughter and flickering candlelight lingering in the shadows of her mind.

Her lover, Atmaj, reclined beside her, his presence as grounding as the ancient stones beneath them. He watched her, a smile playing on his lips as he marvelled at her ethereal beauty—the way the morning light danced across her skin, highlighting the gentle curves of her body. She looked up at him, her eyes shimmering with an otherworldly light, as if the very essence of the jungle pulsed within her.

In an intoxicating blend of playfulness and reverence, she pressed her hands against the stone, arching her back slightly as if to invite the energy of the earth into her. "Come closer," she beckoned softly, her voice a melodic whisper that echoed through the lush surroundings. She seemed to be in a trance, a spirit of the jungle, lost in the sacred space they had created together.

As he approached, Atmaj felt a magnetic pull between them, an unspoken understanding that transcended the physical realm. She spread her legs slightly, an invitation wrapped in vulnerability and trust. "Fulfil my desires," she murmured, her breath hitching with the weight of desire, a delicate balance of love and lust reflected in her eyes.

Atmaj undressed slowly, reverently, as if shedding not just his clothes but also the barriers between them. He felt a rush of warmth course through him, ignited by her openness, the promise of their connection setting his heart racing. As he settled onto the stone beside her, the world around them faded into a gentle hum, leaving only the pulsating rhythm of their hearts.

With careful intention, he joined her, their bodies aligning as he entered her. The initial contact was soft, a melding of souls, and they shared a breath, an electric moment of pure intimacy that stretched into eternity. Atmaj moved slowly at first, cherishing every second, his love flowing through each rhythmic movement. He felt her body respond, the way it arched and welcomed him, a harmony that echoed the wild beauty of the jungle surrounding them.

As passion ignited between them, the tempo of their connection quickened. Each thrust became more fervent, a dance of primal energy that mirrored the life force of the jungle—wild, untamed, and beautifully sacred. They lost themselves in the rhythm, the sounds of their union blending with the symphony of nature, the rustling leaves and distant calls of birds amplifying their love.

In the throes of shared ecstasy, they became one with the universe, a beautiful fusion of love and desire echoing against the ancient stones cradling them. Time seemed to dissolve, leaving only the raw intensity of their connection, a moment that felt both eternal and fleeting, bathed in the glory of the dawn breaking around them. In that sacred space, they were free, two souls dancing in the heart of the jungle.

Chapter 17

The streets of London were abuzz with anticipation as the annual Occult Science Festival took centre stage. This year, the event had garnered even more attention, as Mira, celebrated author and healer, was among its star guests. Her recent book, Time Whisperer, had not only broken records as the bestselling book of the year in 2024 but also sparked global conversations on spirituality, healing, and time-bound energies. Invitations had flooded her way, from TV shows to book tours, yet this festival held a special appeal, promising an audience as curious and spiritually driven as she was.

Mira arrived on the opening day to find herself immediately swept into a whirlwind of activity. The event, held at an elegant historic venue that seemed to meld with the mystique of the occasion, was filled with rows of booths and workshops offering everything from tarot readings to astrology charts, aura photography to seminars on past life exploration.

The first event on Mira's schedule was a lecture in one of the grand halls, where nearly a hundred attendees waited, captivated by the energy she brought to her words. Dressed in an elegant, flowing outfit that gave her an ethereal presence, Mira greeted the room with a gentle smile, feeling at ease among people who shared her passion for the mystical.

Taking the stage, she began with an anecdote from her book, describing the powerful experience that led her to her path as a "time whisperer" and healer. She spoke of the ancient, forgotten wisdom she had discovered through her work with the Akashic records and the intuitive journeys that had guided her in helping souls heal. Mira shared her belief that time was not a straight line, as many assumed, but a complex tapestry, with past, present, and future often overlapping in ways the conscious mind could scarcely imagine.

The room was hushed as she wove through stories of her most intriguing sessions, where people had reclaimed lost parts of themselves through glimpses into their past lives. "Sometimes," she explained, "it's not the future we're afraid of but fragments of a past that still linger, waiting to be acknowledged, healed, and integrated."

She opened the floor to questions, and hands shot up immediately. People wanted to know about her methods, her sources of inspiration, and how she handled the weight of such intense spiritual work. Mira answered thoughtfully, each response carrying the weight of her experience, and she was moved by how earnestly the audience listened.

After the lecture, she was whisked away to a book-signing event. The line stretched down the hallway, with people eager to get a signed copy of Time Whisperer and perhaps a moment of conversation with her. She met readers of all ages, from young women and men eager to explore spirituality to older attendees who felt their journeys were intertwined with hers. Mira's warm smile and genuine interest in each person made the experience unforgettable for those who met her.

Each book she signed was accompanied by a thoughtful dedication, as she paused to ask each person about their journey. Some of them shared personal stories—how her book had helped them reconnect with a lost part of themselves, or how it had inspired them to look at time and memory differently. She often found herself moved by their words, a gentle reminder of why she had written her story in the first place.

The afternoon was reserved for interviews, the first being with a popular podcast host known for exploring themes of spirituality and mysticism. In the intimate setting of a soundproof studio, they began a candid conversation that quickly veered into profound territory. The host, visibly intrigued, asked her about her journey from healer to author, and how she had found the courage to share such vulnerable, personal experiences in her book.

Mira explained that the book had come to her almost as a calling, a way to reach those who, like her, had always felt an inexplicable connection to the unseen realms. She shared that the process had been deeply transformative, that she'd unearthed parts of herself she hadn't known existed until she poured them onto the page. They spoke about the dual nature of time, how events that seem to belong to the past often linger within us, shaping who we are.

During a break, Mira was approached by the podcast's producer, who expressed interest in developing a series based on her ideas, perhaps delving deeper into her sessions, spiritual insights, and the journeys she had taken with others. Mira was intrigued and tentatively agreed, her heart racing at the idea of bringing her work to an even larger audience.

The next interview was with a television crew from an international channel. The interview was set against a dimly lit, luxurious backdrop with intricate tapestries and mystic symbols, designed to evoke a sense of mystery and allure. The interviewer, a well-known figure in the metaphysical community, questioned Mira on her thoughts regarding the intersection of science and spirituality.

Mira spoke with clarity and conviction, noting that while traditional science measured tangible phenomena, spirituality explored the subtle, unseen currents that flowed through existence. "Science and spirituality aren't opposites," she said.

"They are parts of a whole, each helping us understand the universe in different ways."

As the day progressed, Mira joined a panel discussion with other prominent figures in the occult world. Each brought a unique perspective—there was a famed astrologer, a crystal healer, and a medium who specialized in ancestral communication. Mira shared the stage gracefully, contributing her thoughts on the timeless nature of the soul and how she believed that our greatest journey was to remember and reclaim parts of ourselves that transcend lifetimes.

When evening came, the festival's energy shifted to a more intimate setting—a small, candle-lit room where Mira joined a handful of readers and curious minds for a fireside chat. Here, she let down her guard a little, speaking with warmth and humour, sharing the challenges of writing such a book and her dreams of where it could lead. People asked personal questions, and Mira answered them earnestly, feeling deeply connected to everyone who had come to listen and learn.

As the night drew to a close, Mira stepped outside, breathing in the cool London air. She had been immersed in a day filled with magic, not only in the mystical sense but in the way her work had touched others and how they had, in turn, inspired her. The Occult Science Festival had offered her a rare glimpse into the hearts of people who shared her passion and her longing for deeper understanding.

Reflecting on the day, Mira felt a deep satisfaction. Her work was more than a book, more than a bestseller—it was a journey she shared with others, a way to ignite the flame of curiosity and transformation in those who dared to explore the mysteries of time, soul, and self.

Mira, was back from her whirlwind UK tour, steps into her Mysore home, feeling a wave of calm wash over her. The city had been her sanctuary for the past 12 years—a place she first arrived in as a curious student and chose to stay, enchanted by its charm. She built a life here, working as a content writer while nurturing her passion for semi-fiction books. But the pull of the mystical was always strong. Even as a child, she was captivated by the unseen, diving into occult sciences whenever she had the chance. Now a seasoned tarot reader, past-life regression therapist, and author of a bestselling book, she at last found her true calling, blended her gift of storytelling with her deep-rooted connection to the spiritual realm.

Chapter 18

Mira was seated in her sanctuary, a place where time itself seemed to pause. The room was dimly lit, only a single candle flickering with a strange hue, casting shadows that danced like sentient beings on the wall. The fragrance of sage and sandalwood permeated the air as Mira prepared herself for another session. Today, she felt an unusual stirring in her spirit, a sense of anticipation as if something or someone was about to arrive, unlike any entity she had encountered before.

She shuffled her tarot deck slowly, feeling the cool texture of the cards against her fingers. Mira closed her eyes, taking deep, rhythmic breaths, and suddenly, she felt the air around her shift—like the silent hum of a different frequency tuning in.

A cold breeze swept across the room, and when Mira opened her eyes, she was no longer alone. Before her, a translucent figure hovered—a tall, slender being with elongated limbs and an elongated face. It was humanoid but not entirely, its skin shimmering like moonlight reflected on water. The being had large, almond-shaped eyes, glistening with a dark, liquid intelligence. It did not speak with words but transmitted its presence through waves of energy that washed over Mira like ripples in a pond.

Mira, calm yet alert, instinctively knew she was facing an envoy from another realm—a distant planet known to some as Arelia. She had heard whispers of this place in her meditations, a world steeped in crystalline structures and suffused with a blue-green light that bore no resemblance to Earth's sun.

"Why have you come?" Mira asked, her voice gentle but filled with the authority of someone who walks between worlds.

The being tilted its head, and a sound like distant chimes echoed in Mira's mind. It spoke in her thoughts, bypassing language entirely: We are the Lorelians, watchers of the cosmos. We have observed your world through the veil. You are a Whisperer; you can hear us. We seek your counsel.

The statement took Mira by surprise. It was rare for entities to come seeking advice; often, they were lost souls or spirits in need of guidance, but this was different. This was an advanced being, a collective intelligence, approaching her for insight.

"What do you seek to know?" she asked, setting the tarot deck in front of her.

The cards shuffled themselves, as if moved by invisible hands. Three cards fell onto the table: The Star, The Hanged Man, and The Tower. Mira felt a jolt run through her as she read them. It was an omen—a celestial conflict, a great change approaching not just Earth but spanning multiple dimensions.

There is a fracture in the fabric of time, the Lorelian communicated. We sense a disturbance, an echo from your realm that resonates across galaxies. A decision made here ripples outward, threatening the balance. We cannot see its origin; we seek your vision.

Mira's pulse quickened. The energy was heavy with urgency, and she knew this was no ordinary reading. She placed her hand over the cards and closed her eyes, allowing herself to fall deeper into her trance. In the darkness behind her eyelids, she saw a vision: a great chasm opening in a vast sky, streaks of violet and gold lightning cracking through it. She saw beings falling through, caught in a whirlpool of light and shadow.

When she opened her eyes, the Lorelian was watching her intently. It understood without her needing to speak the vision aloud.

You must mend it, it said. Your kind has the power to heal the rift. It starts with a choice—yours or another's. We cannot interfere directly; it is your fate to decide.

Mira felt the weight of the responsibility pressing down on her chest. "I will do what I can," she promised, her voice a whisper, and as quickly as it had arrived, the Lorelian dissipated into thin air, leaving behind only the faint scent of ozone and a single, shimmering strand of ethereal silk that drifted slowly to the ground.

Mira felt the echo of the Lorelian's departure like the fading vibrations of a struck bell, leaving the air thin and charged with energy. She stood still, sensing that the entity had not left entirely—it lingered at the edges of her perception, tethered by a thread of unresolved tension.

The Lorelian's request for help was vague yet laden with a gravity Mira had rarely felt before. A fracture in the fabric of time, it had said. But what did that truly mean? As she pondered, the scent of ozone thickened again, and Mira knew the envoy was reaching out once more. She focused her energy and pulled a veil of light over her inner eye, allowing her spirit to travel. Suddenly, she was no longer in her room.

She found herself standing on a vast, crystalline plain. The ground beneath her feet shimmered like a frozen lake, casting iridescent reflections that danced with a life of their own. Overhead, a sky of pale lavender arched infinitely, dotted with clusters of stars that seemed to pulse like living hearts. This was Arelia, a world she had only glimpsed in her deepest meditative states. It was a place where light was not merely illumination but a living, breathing entity that carried messages across the sky like whispers in a breeze.

Before her, the Lorelian materialized once more, its form more solid now, less ghostly. It was as if the proximity to its home had granted it a fuller presence. The being raised a long, slender arm and gestured toward the horizon, where the crystalline plain seemed to fracture like shattered glass. Dark, jagged lines rippled through the otherwise perfect landscape, oozing a thick, smoke-like mist.

This is the wound, the Lorelian said, its voice a harmonious blend of many tones. The fracture spreads, a consequence of choices made beyond our realm. It is not our doing, but we cannot heal it alone. Your kind, your world, has set this chain of events in motion.

Mira stepped closer, feeling the cold, magnetic pull of the rift. It felt alive, pulsating with a chaotic energy that seemed to devour the light around it. "What happened here?" she asked, her voice barely a whisper in the sacred silence of Arelia.

Time has become unstable, the Lorelian explained, its eyes reflecting the fractured light. A decision made on Earth, an imbalance between fate and free will, has created a ripple effect. Your actions, your world's interference in the flow of time, have caused this tear.

Mira felt a cold wave of realization wash over her. It dawned on her that the choice she had made—one that seemed inconsequential at the time—had been the catalyst. It was a reading she had done months ago, for a high-ranking government official, a man desperate to alter his fate. Mira had guided him, sensing the urgency and danger surrounding his choices. She had helped him see the paths ahead, steering him away from disaster, but in doing so, she had unwittingly altered the natural flow of events, creating a ripple that had spread far beyond Earth.

"I didn't know," Mira said, her voice tinged with regret. "I didn't realize the consequences of that reading."

No one could have known, the Lorelian replied, its tone gentle despite the gravity of the situation. But now you must help us mend the tear. It requires a sacrifice—an offering of time itself. You must return a fragment of the life force you borrowed when you altered the path.

Mira took a deep breath. She understood what was being asked of her. Time was a precious commodity, one that flowed like a river, never to be reclaimed once lost. To mend the rift, she would need to offer a piece of her own lifespan, a sacrifice of the years she had left—a steep price, but one she knew she must pay.

Without hesitation, she nodded. "Show me what I need to do."

The Lorelian extended its hand, and a sphere of pure, white light appeared between them, hovering in the air. It pulsed with a rhythm that matched the beat of Mira's heart. This is the core of the fracture. It has latched onto a piece of your time, siphoning it like a leech. You must give it willingly, let it take what it needs, and the balance will be restored.

Mira closed her eyes, feeling the warmth of the sphere as it floated closer to her. She reached out and touched it, feeling a jolt of energy course through her body. In that moment, she saw flashes of her own life—the days spent laughing with her children, the quiet mornings of meditation, the future she had envisioned for herself. She felt a pang of sorrow but let it pass, focusing instead on the greater good.

"I offer this willingly," she whispered. The sphere absorbed her words, and a sharp, searing pain shot through her chest as if a piece of her soul had been torn away. The pain was brief but profound, leaving her breathless.

The fracture in the crystalline plain shuddered, then slowly began to mend. The jagged lines receded, knitting themselves back together until the landscape was once again pristine and whole. The dark mist evaporated, replaced by a gentle, luminescent glow that spread across the horizon like the dawn.

Mira staggered back, feeling the drain of her life force. The Lorelian stepped closer, placing a hand on her shoulder—a gesture of gratitude, she realized.

You have done what we could not, it said. The rift is healed, and the balance is restored. But know this: time is fragile. Every choice reverberates across worlds. We are all bound by the threads of fate.

Mira nodded, too exhausted to speak. She felt herself being pulled back, the landscape of Arelia fading into a blur of light and shadow. When she opened her eyes again, she was back in her sanctuary, the candle still burning low on the table. She looked down and noticed a new line etched into her palm, a mark left behind from her encounter—a reminder of the time she had given away.

As she slumped into her chair, Mira felt an overwhelming sense of peace. The room was filled with the lingering essence of the Lorelian, a soft, melodic hum that resonated in her bones. She knew she had done the right thing, even if it had cost her dearly.

And as she sat there, breathing slowly, she realized something profound: she had touched the very fabric of time itself, and in doing so, she had become a part of its eternal dance—a Whisperer not just of the past, but of all things that ever were and ever would be.

This experience marked a turning point for Mira, a deepening of her powers and her understanding of the delicate web that binds all existence. From now on, she would tread more carefully, knowing that even the smallest whisper could echo across the universe.

Chapter 19

It was a Friday night in Bengaluru, and Mira had been coaxed into a rare night out with her friends. Her friend Leena, a vibrant, free-spirited woman with a penchant for spontaneous adventures, insisted they celebrate the starting of the weekend with drinks and dancing. It had been a long time since they last met.

The pub they chose was a quirky, dimly lit place tucked away in the labyrinthine streets of Church Street. It was an eclectic mix of old and new—brick walls adorned with neon signs, vintage leather booths paired with industrial bar stools, and a jukebox playing a blend of old-school rock and contemporary pop. The place was packed, filled with the buzz of laughter, clinking glasses, and the hum of conversation.

Mira walked in with her four friends: Leena, Raj, Anu, and Vikram. Leena was already leading the group toward the bar, her curly hair bouncing with every step. Anu, the soft-spoken but sharp-eyed historian, was quietly observing the crowd, while Vikram, the sceptic of the group, was trying to hide his surprise at the colourful scene. Raj, a tech geek who always looked slightly out of place at such gatherings, seemed both thrilled and nervous.

As they settled in at a high table near the dance floor, Mira felt a strange sensation, like a static charge prickling at the back of her neck. She scanned the room casually, her eyes sweeping over the sea of faces. That's when she noticed him—a man standing at the far end of the bar, his back to her. He looked like any other regular: tall, dressed in a fitted black turtleneck and dark jeans, with tousled dark hair.

But something was off.

Mira's senses were heightened from years of practice. She could feel the energy emanating from people; she knew when someone was troubled, when they were hiding something, or when they were simply intoxicated. This man, however, radiated an entirely different kind of energy—cold, sharp, and distinctly not human.

She nudged Anu and nodded subtly in the man's direction. "Do you see him?"

Anu squinted, then shook her head. "What do you mean? He looks normal."

Mira leaned closer, her voice barely a whisper. "He's not normal. Look closely."

As if on cue, the man turned, meeting Mira's gaze directly. His eyes were dark, almost black, but there was no reflection, no light within them. They were like deep, endless wells, absorbing rather than reflecting the light around him. He smiled—a slow, deliberate smile that didn't reach his eyes.

Mira's breath caught. The man lifted his glass in a mock toast, as if acknowledging her scrutiny.

"Who's that?" Vikram asked, following her line of sight. He seemed oblivious to the man's odd demeanour.

"I don't know," Mira replied slowly, "but he's… different."

Raj, overhearing the conversation, laughed. "Oh no, Mira. Don't tell me you've found another spirit or alien. We're here to relax, not work."

Leena grinned, leaning in. "Maybe he's a vampire! Or one of your interdimensional friends. Go talk to him, Mira. It'll be fun."

Mira rolled her eyes but couldn't shake the feeling of unease. She decided to humour her friends and make her way over to the bar, where the man was now leaning casually, sipping his drink. As she approached, she could feel the air around him change— like the temperature had dropped a few degrees.

She stopped a few feet away, giving him a polite smile. "Interesting night, isn't it?"

"Indeed," he replied. His voice was smooth, almost melodic, but there was an undertone to it that made Mira's skin crawl. "You've been watching me, Mira."

Her eyes widened slightly. "How do you know my name?"

He chuckled, a sound that seemed almost too perfect, like it was practiced. "You're quite well-known in certain circles—both human and otherwise."

Mira's heart skipped a beat. She had suspected he wasn't human, but to have it confirmed so bluntly took her by surprise. "What are you?" she asked, dropping the pretence.

He tilted his head, considering her with an amused expression. "I'm a traveller, just passing through. This city, this planet—it's a fascinating little corner of the universe, don't you think?"

"Where are you from?" Mira pressed, her voice barely above a whisper now.

"Somewhere you've never heard of," he said, his smile widening. "But if you must know, let's just say it's not on any map your people have drawn."

"Why are you here?" Mira asked. She noticed his eyes flicker briefly, like the screen of a malfunctioning television.

"Why is anyone here?" he countered, spreading his arms wide. "For the experience, of course. To observe. To understand." He leaned closer, and she caught a whiff of something metallic, like the scent of a freshly struck coin. "And sometimes, to meddle."

Mira felt a shiver run down her spine. "Are you here to meddle tonight?"

He laughed, a sound that made the hair on her arms stand on end. "Not tonight. Tonight, I'm just enjoying the show." He nodded toward her friends, who were laughing and clinking their glasses. "They're so full of life. It's intoxicating, isn't it?"

Mira realized then what he was doing. "You're feeding off their energy," she said, her voice sharp.

"Feeding is such a crude word," he replied with a smirk. "Let's say… sampling. You have to admit, they won't miss a little bit of their vitality, not after a night like this."

Mira's hand instinctively went to her tarot deck, tucked safely in her purse. She pulled out a single card without looking. It was The Fool, a card of new beginnings but also of naive, reckless energy. She held it up for him to see.

"Are you playing the fool, or are we?" she asked, her tone edged with challenge.

He looked at the card and laughed, a deep, resonant sound that filled the room and seemed to warp the air around them. "Ah, but that's the question, isn't it? Maybe we're all just fools in this cosmic dance."

With a wink, he downed the rest of his drink, set the glass on the bar, and began to walk away. Mira felt the air lighten as he left, like a pressure valve had been released.

Just before he reached the door, he turned back one last time. "You're an interesting one, Mira. I'll be seeing you again. Perhaps next time, I'll bring some friends."

And with that, he was gone, slipping out into the night as if he had never been there. Mira stood at the bar, her heart racing, the Fool card still in her hand. She knew he wasn't bluffing. This was just the beginning of something far stranger than she had ever imagined.

She rejoined her friends, who were oblivious to the entire encounter. Raj was busy arguing with Leena about the best song on the jukebox, and Anu was telling Vikram about a new historical theory. Mira slipped the Fool card back into her deck, feeling the weight of what had just happened.

"Everything okay?" Anu asked, noticing Mira's slightly dazed expression.

Mira smiled, shaking her head in disbelief. "Yeah, everything's fine," she said, laughing to herself. "Just met an old friend, that's all."

But as she looked toward the door, she couldn't help but wonder how many more of these "old friends" were out there, watching, waiting, blending in with the human crowd.

Chapter 20

The air carried a faint, salty scent as Mira stepped barefoot on the golden sands of the private beach near Kundapura. The sun, now sinking towards the horizon, cast a warm, orange glow that painted everything in shades of amber and gold. Mira's friend, Suraj, had insisted she join him for a few days at his family's coastal retreat—a sprawling villa hidden away among coconut groves and wild bougainvillea. He knew how much she needed this escape after the intense months of travel and healing work that had drained her.

The villa itself was a sanctuary of sorts, with whitewashed walls, large verandas, and hammocks strung between swaying palms. Mira had found it to be the perfect cocoon, a place where she could breathe deeply and reconnect with herself. Here, she was free from the noise of the city, the constant requests for readings, and the heavy energies that often lingered around her clients. Here, she could simply be.

As she walked along the beach, the cool December breeze ruffled her hair, carrying the sound of waves crashing gently against the shore. The sand was still warm under her feet, a comforting sensation that made her feel rooted to the earth. The sea was a deep blue, almost indigo, with white-tipped waves rolling in rhythmically. She watched as the sun dipped lower, casting a trail of shimmering light across the water like a pathway leading to another realm.

Mira had spent the past few days in a blissful routine of simplicity: waking up with the sunrise, sipping freshly brewed filter coffee while gazing at the endless expanse of the Arabian Sea, and indulging in the rich, spicy flavours of local Konkani cuisine. She loved the crispy neer dosa paired with coconut chutney, the tangy fish curry cooked with kokum, and the sweet, melt-in-the-mouth obbattu served with a drizzle of ghee. Every meal was a reminder of the deep, earthy flavours of this land, nourishing her not just physically but spiritually as well.

Suraj had been a gracious host, understanding her need for both companionship and solitude. They often took long walks together, talking about everything and nothing—the universe, the mysteries of time, old memories from their college days. And when Mira needed time alone, he knew to leave her be, retreating to the villa with a book or to prepare another one of his delicious coastal delicacies.

Today, Mira had chosen to walk alone, seeking the quiet whisper of the waves as her only companion. She could feel the sea's energy wrapping around her like a gentle embrace, washing away the fatigue and the lingering sadness she hadn't realized she was still carrying. The sea had always been her refuge—a place where she could hear her own thoughts clearly, where the noise of the world faded into the background.

She found a smooth, flat rock near the water's edge and sat down, pulling her knees to her chest and watching as the waves rolled in, kissing the shore before retreating once more. The sun had almost disappeared now, leaving behind a sky streaked with pink and purple, a masterpiece of colours that seemed to reflect Mira's own shifting emotions. She closed her eyes, breathing deeply, feeling the cool spray of the sea mist against her face.

Mira's mind drifted to her writing, the stories she had begun to weave while staying here. The coastal air seemed to spark her creativity, each breeze carrying with it the whisper of a new idea. Her notebook was already filled with sketches, ideas for new chapters, and fragments of poems she hadn't felt inspired to write in years. The sea had a way of opening her heart, of making her feel safe enough to delve into the deepest parts of her psyche and pull out the words that lay hidden there.

As the twilight deepened, Mira felt a shift in the air—an almost imperceptible change, like the moment before a thunderstorm when the world seemed to hold its breath. She opened her eyes and glanced down at the beach. The shoreline was empty except for a few scattered shells and the occasional driftwood, yet she couldn't shake the feeling that she wasn't entirely alone.

She stood up, dusting the sand off her dress, and began to walk back toward the villa. The wind had picked up, rustling the palm leaves and carrying with it the faint, melodic sound of a temple bell ringing somewhere in the distance. It was then that she saw a figure far down the beach, silhouetted against the last light of the day. The person seemed to be standing still, gazing out at the sea, unmoving despite the strengthening breeze.

Mira paused, squinting to get a better look. There was something oddly familiar about the stance, the way the figure's head tilted slightly as if listening to the whispers of the waves. It wasn't Suraj—that much she was sure of. He had gone to the village market earlier, planning to return only after sunset. And yet, this figure exuded a presence that was unmistakable, an energy that

Mira's senses recognized before her mind could make sense of it.

The figure turned slowly, as if sensing her gaze, and even from this distance, Mira could see a faint smile—a smile that wasn't threatening, but it was knowing, like the smile of someone who sees beyond the surface, someone who exists outside the ordinary flow of time.

Mira took a step forward, then stopped herself. Her heart was pounding now, a rush of excitement mixed with caution. She had encountered many beings before—spirits, entities from other dimensions—but there was something different about this one. The air around her seemed to vibrate with a low hum, a sound she could almost feel rather than hear.

The figure raised a hand, not in a wave but in a gesture of acknowledgment, and then, as if dissolving into the twilight itself, it vanished. One moment it was there, and the next, it was gone—leaving behind only the faintest trace of energy, like the aftertaste of a strong, unfamiliar spice.

Mira stood there for a moment, feeling the dampness of the sea breeze on her skin, her mind racing. She knew she had just experienced a glimpse of something profound, a presence that was both a visitor and a guide. It wasn't a spirit, not in the traditional sense. It felt more ancient, more elemental—as if the sea itself had taken a human form to greet her.

Slowly, she turned and continued her walk back to the villa, the excitement buzzing through her veins. She knew she had more questions than answers, but she also knew that this was just the beginning of something extraordinary. This beach, this sacred land, was awakening something within her, drawing her into a deeper mystery that she was only beginning to understand.

The night would bring its own revelations, she thought with a smile. And she was ready, more ready than she had ever been, to embrace whatever whispers the sea would bring her way.

The evening sky was a deep indigo, and the waves whispered their secrets to the shore as Mira sat on the terrace of the villa, sipping a cup of ginger tea. She could feel the wind shifting, bringing with it a different kind of energy—one that felt heavy, laden with the weight of emotions she hadn't expected to encounter on this trip.

She had sensed it from the first moment she arrived at Suraj's family retreat. It was subtle, like a distant hum, but unmistakable. There was tension lurking beneath the surface of this beautiful coastal sanctuary, a tension she could feel in the way Suraj's wife, Ranjini, avoided direct eye contact and kept her voice light, almost forced. Mira's intuition whispered that something wasn't right, but she chose to wait, to let the truth reveal itself in its own time.

That evening, as the moon began its ascent, Mira received a text message from Ranjini: Can we talk? I need a session. Tonight, if possible.

Mira replied immediately, telling her to come up to the terrace. She prepared her space, lighting a stick of sandalwood incense and shuffling her tarot deck, the familiar weight of the cards grounding her in the moment. She had a feeling this session would be different, not the usual readings she performed for guidance or reassurance. This felt urgent, raw.

Ranjini arrived a few minutes later, her steps hesitant, eyes darting nervously. She wore a simple white kurta, her hair pulled back in a loose braid, but her face was pale, and her eyes were rimmed with exhaustion. She looked like a woman who hadn't slept properly in weeks.

"Please, sit," Mira said, gesturing to the cushioned chair opposite her. "Take a deep breath. You're safe here."

Ranjini managed a shaky smile, but it crumbled almost immediately. She sank into the chair, clasping her hands tightly in her lap, knuckles turning white. Mira watched her carefully, tuning into the energy that radiated off her like waves. Anger, guilt, sadness—they all swirled together in a chaotic dance.

"I don't know where to start," Ranjini admitted, her voice barely a whisper. "Everything feels… wrong. And I can't make sense of it."

"Take your time," Mira said gently. "Let's begin with whatever feels the most pressing for you."

Ranjini looked down, twisting her wedding ring around her finger. "It's my marriage," she said, her voice breaking. "I love Suraj, but I don't know if he loves me anymore. We've been together for years, but now… it feels like we're strangers. He's distant, always busy, and when he does speak to me, it's as if he's speaking to someone else. I'm angry at him, but I'm also angry at myself. I can't tell if I've pushed him away or if he's already gone."

Tears welled up in her eyes, and she wiped them away quickly, as if ashamed of her vulnerability. Mira handed her a tissue and gave her a moment to compose herself.

"Ranjini," Mira began softly, "I sense that there's more beneath the surface. You're not just angry; you're carrying a lot of guilt, too. What do you feel guilty about?"

Ranjini's shoulders slumped, and she let out a shaky breath. "I'm guilty because I've been thinking about leaving him. But at the same time, I'm terrified of what that would mean. What if I'm the problem? What if I'm the one who's broken?"

Mira nodded slowly, absorbing her words. She reached for her tarot deck and began shuffling, feeling the familiar energy of the cards as they passed through her fingers. She asked Ranjini to cut the deck and then drew three cards, laying them out in a line on the small table between them.

The first card was The Moon, symbolizing illusions, hidden truths, and the subconscious mind. The second was The Three of Swords, a card of heartbreak, betrayal, and deep emotional pain. The third was The Tower, representing sudden upheaval, a collapse of old structures, and a dramatic change.

Ranjini stared at the cards, her face going pale. "What does this mean?"

Mira took a deep breath, feeling the weight of the reading settle into her bones. "It means you've been living in the shadow of something hidden, something you haven't been willing to face. The Moon tells me that there are illusions in your marriage, things that you and Suraj haven't been honest about with each other—or even with yourselves. The Three of Swords shows the pain you're both feeling, a wound that hasn't been healed, perhaps one that hasn't even been acknowledged. And The Tower... Well), it's the card of transformation. It signifies a breaking point. Whatever is happening now, it can't continue the way it is. Change is coming, whether you're ready for it or not."

Ranjini's breath hitched, and she pressed a hand to her chest, as if trying to hold herself together. "Is it over?" she asked, her voice choked. "Is my marriage going to end?"

Mira leaned forward, her eyes gentle but firm. "I can't answer that for you. The cards don't dictate your future—they show you the energy of the present and the potential paths ahead. The Tower is a sign that something needs to be rebuilt, but what you choose to rebuild is up to you. This is a chance for you to confront the truth, whatever that truth may be."

Ranjini's expression crumpled, and she buried her face in her hands, sobbing quietly. Mira placed a comforting hand on her shoulder, giving her the space to release her emotions.

"Ranjini," Mira said softly once the sobs had subsided, "you need to stop blaming yourself for everything. There are two people in this relationship, and both of you have contributed to where you are now. You need to have a real conversation with Suraj, an honest one, without the masks you've both been wearing. But before you do that, I want to help you centre yourself, to find your strength again."

Ranjini looked up, her eyes red but filled with a spark of hope. "How?"

"I'll teach you a few grounding techniques," Mira said. "Meditation will help you reconnect with your inner voice, so you can hear your own truth clearly. And I want you to practice these every day. This isn't about fixing your marriage right now—it's about fixing your relationship with yourself. The stronger you become, the clearer your path will be."

Ranjini nodded, wiping away the last of her tears. "Thank you, Mira. I don't know what I expected when I came here, but… this feels like the first step."

Mira smiled warmly. "I'll be here for you. And when you leave, we'll set up regular video calls. I want you to know that you're not alone in this. But I also want to be honest with you—I can't promise you that your marriage will survive this, and I won't give you false hope. What I can promise is that I'll help you find the strength to face whatever comes next."

Ranjini reached across the table and squeezed Mira's hand. "I trust you," she whispered. "I don't know why, but I do."

"That's your intuition speaking," Mira replied with a knowing smile. "It's about time you started listening to it."

They ended the session with a quiet meditation, the sound of the sea blending with their rhythmic breathing. As Ranjini left, Mira felt a deep sense of responsibility, but also a sense of purpose. This was why she did what she did—not to provide easy answers, but to guide people through the shadows of their own lives and help them find the light within.

And as she watched Ranjini walk back toward the villa, Mira knew that this was just the beginning of a long, difficult journey. But it was a journey Ranjini was finally ready to take, and Mira would be there, every step of the way, guiding her like a steady hand in the dark.

The next morning, Mira awoke before sunrise. The air was cool, and the sound of the waves created a soothing rhythm that matched her steady breath. She could feel the energy of the previous night lingering—a heavy, unresolved presence that settled like a cloud over the villa. Mira knew the session with Ranjini had only scratched the surface. There was something deeper, something Ranjini hadn't been ready to say aloud.

Later that day, after a quiet breakfast with Suraj and Ranjini, Mira found a moment alone on the veranda. The sea breeze tousled her hair as she shuffled her tarot deck, feeling the familiar weight of the cards. She often turned to them not just for her clients but for herself, as a way of connecting to her intuition. She sensed that today would bring another opportunity to help Ranjini, but she needed to be prepared.

Just as she was laying out a few cards for a personal reading, she heard a soft voice behind her. "Mira, do you have a moment?"

It was Ranjini, looking hesitant but more composed than the previous night. Her eyes still held a shadow of worry, but there was a new determination in them.

"Of course," Mira said, gesturing for her to sit. "I was just thinking about you. Would you like to continue our conversation from yesterday?"

Ranjini nodded, taking a seat opposite Mira. She glanced down at the table, where a few cards were already spread out. The High Priestess, The Eight of Cups, and The Five of Pentacles. Mira noticed the flicker of recognition in Ranjini's eyes and waited.

"What do these cards mean?" Ranjini asked, her voice cautious, as if afraid to know the answer.

Mira studied the cards, feeling a surge of insight. "The High Priestess represents intuition, hidden knowledge, and secrets kept below the surface. The Eight of Cups speaks of walking away, leaving something behind that no longer serves you. And The Five of Pentacles... Well, it's a card of hardship, loss, and feeling abandoned. It's about being left out in the cold, emotionally or physically."

Ranjini's face paled, and she looked away, out toward the horizon. "That's exactly how I feel," she admitted quietly. "Like I've been left behind, and I don't know why. I keep blaming myself, wondering what I did wrong."

Mira leaned forward, her voice gentle but probing. "Ranjini, I don't believe you've shared the full story with me. There's more here, isn't there? Something you're afraid to say out loud?"

Ranjini's eyes filled with tears, but she held them back, swallowing hard. "It's not that I don't want to tell you," she whispered. "It's just… I don't even know where to begin. And I'm afraid if I say it, it'll make it real."

Mira placed her hand over Ranjini's, squeezing gently. "You don't have to say it. Let me ask the cards. If I see the truth in them, you won't have to explain everything. You can just listen and decide how you want to proceed."

Ranjini nodded, her shoulders sagging with relief. It was as if the burden of over-explaining had been lifted, and for the first time, she felt seen, understood.

Mira took a deep breath and shuffled the deck, closing her eyes as she focused on the question in her mind: What is the real source of discord in Ranjini's marriage? She drew three cards, laying them out with a quiet sense of reverence.

The first card was The Devil—a symbol of bondage, temptation, and unhealthy attachments. The second was The Seven of Swords, a card of deceit, betrayal, and hidden agendas. The third was The Ten of Wands, representing an overwhelming burden, carrying more than one's fair share of the load.

Mira's eyes softened as she looked up at Ranjini. "I'm going to tell you what I see, and I want you to know that this isn't about judgment. It's about understanding what's happening so you can make the right choices for yourself."

Ranjini nodded, her hands trembling slightly. "Go on."

"The Devil card tells me there's an element of control and manipulation in your relationship," Mira began slowly. "It could be coming from you, from Suraj, or both of you in different ways. It speaks of patterns that are toxic—patterns that keep you bound, even when you know they're hurting you."

Ranjini's lips parted, but she didn't say anything, her face a mask of shock and recognition.

"The Seven of Swords," Mira continued, "is a card of deception. There's a lack of honesty here, and I don't just mean with each other. It's about self-deception as well. You've both been pretending everything is fine, ignoring the cracks, but deep down, you know the truth. There's been betrayal—whether it's emotional or physical, I can't say for certain, but there's a wound here that hasn't healed."

Tears spilled down Ranjini's cheeks now, and she nodded silently, her body shaking with silent sobs. Mira handed her a tissue but didn't stop. She knew she needed to push through, to reveal the full picture.

"The Ten of Wands," she said softly, "tells me you've been carrying the weight of this relationship on your shoulders. You're exhausted, Ranjini. You've taken on too much, trying to hold it all together, trying to fix things that aren't entirely yours to fix. And it's breaking you down."

Ranjini let out a choked sob, covering her face with her hands. "It's true," she whispered. "It's all true. Suraj… he's been distant for so long. I found messages, months ago. Flirtatious, inappropriate. He denied it at first, saying it was just a misunderstanding, that it meant nothing. But I knew, deep down, I knew."

Mira felt a deep sadness settle in her chest, the pain of so many women she had met over the years reflected in Ranjini's eyes. "I'm so sorry you've had to carry this alone," she said quietly. "But now that it's out in the open, we can start to address it. The cards show that this is a time of reckoning. You have a choice to make, and it won't be easy. But you don't have to decide right now."

Ranjini wiped her tears, looking at Mira with a mixture of gratitude and desperation. "What should I do? How do I even begin to heal from this?"

Mira took her hands, holding them firmly. "First, you need to stop blaming yourself. This isn't your fault. You can't control Suraj's actions, only your own. I want you to focus on grounding yourself—meditate every day, practice deep breathing, and reconnect with your own inner voice. And remember, you don't have to make any major decisions immediately. Give yourself the space to feel, to process."

Mira paused, sensing Ranjini's anxiety easing slightly. "I'll be here for you," she added. "And when I go back home, we'll keep in touch through video calls. I want to help you navigate this, not by giving you false hope, but by preparing you for whatever comes next. This is your journey, Ranjini, and I'm honoured to walk alongside you as you find your way."

Ranjini squeezed Mira's hands, her expression filled with a fragile but unmistakable hope. "Thank you," she whispered. "I've never felt so seen, so understood. I think… I think I'm ready to face this now."

And as the sun dipped lower in the sky, casting long shadows across the veranda, Mira knew that a small but significant shift had occurred. Ranjini had found a sliver of strength, a tiny spark of resolve that had been buried under the weight of her pain. It was the beginning of her journey to healing—a journey Mira knew would be long and painful, but one she was determined to help guide, step by step, card by card, truth by truth.

Chapter 21

The sun hung high in the December sky, casting golden light over the endless blue of the Arabian Sea. Mira felt the cool, silky water envelop her as she dove beneath a wave, her body moving effortlessly through the surf. The sea was her element. She felt alive and free here, each stroke a meditation, each breath filling her lungs with the salty air that made her feel more grounded and present than she had felt in months.

Her vibrant bikini, a recent purchase from London, hugged her figure with a playful elegance. The bright colours and sleek design contrasted beautifully with the turquoise water, making her feel like a part of the sea itself. As she surfaced, pushing her wet hair back from her face, she noticed Suraj standing at the edge of the water, watching her. For a moment, their eyes met, and Mira felt a flicker of something she couldn't quite place, a gaze that lingered a bit too long, his eyes darker than she remembered, filled with an intensity that was unfamiliar. She hesitated, a strange sensation creeping into her chest, but then she waved, forcing herself to smile, pushing aside the discomfort. "Come in," Suraj! she called out, her voice light and teasing, "the water is perfect." Suraj grinned back, already pulling off his shirt.

He kicked off his sandals and dropped his shorts onto the sand, leaving only his swang trunks as he sprinted into the waves. Mira laughed as he splashed toward her, the tension from a moment ago dissolving in the playful spray of water. They swam together, diving and racing like children, the world outside the waves forgotten. Suraj showed her a few tricks-how to time her dive with the swell of the waves, how to float effortlessly on her back as if she was weightless. Mira found herself relaxing, enjoying the spontaneity of the moment.

An hour passed before Mira felt the familiar gnaw of hunger. She floated on her back, looking up at the sky, feeling the sun warm her face. "Suraj, I am starving". She complained with a playful whine, letting her feet sink beneath her as she treaded water. "Can we please head back? I need food".

The sea was alive around them, the waves rising and falling in a rhythm that seemed to sync with their mood.

Suraj swam closer, grinning like a mischievous schoolboy. Just a few more minutes, "Mira. You are such a lightweight". She rolled her eyes, pretending to pout. "Fine, but if I faint from hunger, it's your fault'. With a sudden burst of energy, Suraj swam behind her, wrapping his strong arms around her waist. Before she could react, he lifted her effortlessly, cradling her against his chest. Mira squealed in surprise, laughing, "Put me down, you idiot", she protested, squirming in his grip. "Not until we are back on shore", he declared. His voice was light, but tinged with something deeper, an undercurrent she couldn't quite place. Mira felt the heat of his skin against her, the press of his chest and for a fleeting moment, she was aware of how close they were. It was just a playful moment between old friends, she told herself, and yet there was a strange, lingering tension that seemed to wrap itself around them like the seaweed drifting in the current. He carried her like that, all the way to shore, wading through the shallows as the water dripped from their bodies. Mira was still laughing as he reached the beach and set her down on the wet sand.

But the moment her feet touched the ground, she noticed a change. The playfulness had vanished from Suraj's face. He stood there, just inches away from her, his expression intense, almost pained. His eyes searched her face as if trying to find something, to say something he couldn't find the words for. "Suraj?" she asked, her laughter fading into confusion, "Are you okay?" For a heartbeat, he didn't respond. He just stared at her, his dark eyes locked into hers.

Then, before she could react, he leaned in, cupping her face with both hands and kissed her—hard. The world seemed to stop. Mira's eyes flew open, shock rippling through her body like an electric current. This was no gentle, hesitant kiss. It was desperate, urgent, filled with a raw intensity that stole her breath away. She felt his lips crushing against hers, the salt of the sea mingling with the taste of his mouth, his strong hands gripping her as if she were the only anchor in a storm. Mira's mind went blank for a moment. Overwhelmed by the suddenness of it, she tried to pull away, pushing against his chest, but Suraj didn't let go. He held her tighter, his body pressing against hers, pinning her against the soft, shifting sand. It felt as though he were a man possessed, driven by a need he had kept buried for far too long. Stop! She tried to say, but her voice was muffled against his lips. She pushed harder, using all her strength, but Suraj was strong, his grip unyielding. Her heart pounded in her chest, not just from the exertion, but from the wave of emotions crashing over her, confusion, fear, anger, and something else she couldn't name, something dark and forbidden that flickered at the edge of her consciousness.

When he finally pulled away, they were both gasping for breath. Suraj's face was a mix of anguish and desire, a raw, open wound she had never seen before. He stepped back, his hands falling to his sides, as if he were suddenly aware of what he had done. Mira, I, he began, his voice hoarse, but she cut him off, stepping back, holding up her hands as if to ward him off. Suraj, what the hell was that? She demanded, her voice shaking, her lips still tingling from the force of his kiss. She could feel her own pulse racing, her mind struggling to process what had just happened. She looked at, he looked at her, his eyes filled with a deep, unspoken pain. "I'm sorry," he whispered, but it wasn't just an apology, it was a confession, a plea, a release of something he had been holding back for years.

Mira's hands flew to her lips as if trying to erase the memory of his touch. You can't just…," She stopped herself, breathing hard, trying to find the right words. "You cannot do that, Suraj. I'm your friend. I trusted you."

"I know," he said, his voice breaking. "I know, but you don't understand. I have tried so hard to push it away, to ignore it. But being here, seeing you like this, I couldn't stop myself. I have never felt this way about anyone, Mira, not even Ranjini."

The mention of his wife's name was like a slap across the face. Mira's shock gave way to a cold, biting anger. "This isn't about me, Suraj," she snapped. " This is about you, and it is about Ranjini too. You can't drag me into whatever mess is happening in your marriage." He flinched as if her words had physically hurt him. "You are right," he said quietly. "You are absolutely right." I am so sorry, Mira, I don't know what came over me."

Mira took a deep breath, trying to steady herself. She could still taste him on her lips, could still feel the imprint of his hands on her skin. It made her feel vulnerable, exposed in a way she had never been before. "We need to talk," she said, her voice softer now, but still firm. "But not here, not like this. I need time to process whatever this is."

He nodded, stepping back further, giving her space. "I understand. Take all the time you need. I will go." And with that, he turned and walked away. His shoulders slumped, leaving Mira standing alone on the beach. The wave lapped at her feet. She watched him go, feeling a mix of emotions so complex she couldn't even begin to unravel them. All she knew was that something had shifted between them, something irrevocable.

It was late. The villa had fallen silent, the only sound the distant crashing of waves against the shore. Mira sat in her room, the soft lamplight casting a golden glow over the pages of her notebook. She had been writing, trying to capture the emotions of the day, but her mind kept drifting back to the beach, to the look in Suraj's eyes after he kissed her. There was a sadness there, a deep well of pain she had never seen before. It left her feeling unsettled, unable to find the peace she had hoped this retreat would bring.

A sudden knock at the door startled her. It was loud, urgent, almost frantic. Mira's heart skipped a beat. She glanced at the clock—past midnight. Who could it be at this hour?

She opened the door cautiously, and there stood Suraj. He looked dishevelled, his eyes bloodshot, his breath carrying the unmistakable scent of alcohol. He was slumped against the doorframe, a broken man barely holding himself up.

"Suraj?" Mira whispered, shocked to see him in this state. "What happened? Oh my God

He didn't answer. Instead, he stepped inside, closing the door behind him. He looked at her with a mixture of desperation and sorrow, his face a mask of raw, unfiltered pain. Tears welled up in his eyes, and he sank to his knees, burying his face in his hands.

"Mira, I'm so sorry," he sobbed, his voice choked with emotion. "I've messed everything up. Please... help me." His eyes taking in the room, the dim light, the transparent night dress she wore that clung to her curves, leaning little to the imagination. He swallowed hard, visibly struggling with his own emotions. "Mira, I don't want to hurt you, and I don't want to cross a line again, but I can't keep pretending. I can't pretend that I don't feel what I feel anymore."

Mira knelt down beside him, her own heart breaking at the sight of her friend in such agony. She placed a hand on his shoulder, trying to comfort him. "Suraj, talk to me. What's going on? You're scaring me."

He lifted his head, tears streaming down his cheeks. "It's Ranjini," he whispered. "It's everything. My marriage… my life… I've destroyed it all. And tonight, what I did to you… I've crossed a line I never should have crossed."

Mira felt a lump rise in her throat. The memory of his kiss flashed before her eyes, the way he had looked at her, like she was the only lifeline he had left. She knew this wasn't just about desire—it was about escape, about reaching out for something he thought he had lost forever.

"Suraj," she said softly, taking his hand in hers. "You need to be honest with me now. What's really going on? Why are you here like this, tonight?"

He squeezed her hand as if it were his last grip on reality. "Because I've loved you, Mira," he said, his voice breaking. "I've loved you for years, even when I married Ranjini. I thought I could make it work, that I could forget about you, but I can't. I never could." Suraj let out a shuddering breath, lowering his head until their foreheads touched.

My marriage ended a long time ago, he said softly. We just haven't admitted it yet. I have been holding on to something that's already gone because I was afraid of what it would mean to let go. But I can't deny this anymore. I want you, Mira. I have always wanted you.

Mira felt the air leave her lungs, a painful realization settling in her chest. The signs had been there all along—his protectiveness, the way he looked at her, the lingering touches that she had brushed off as platonic. But now, hearing the words spoken aloud, it felt like a weight she hadn't been prepared to bear.

"Suraj, you can't say these things," she whispered, her voice thick with emotion. "I'm your friend. I love you, but not in the way you want me to. You're married. This isn't right."

"I know," he said, his voice hoarse. "I know it's wrong, but I can't help how I feel. Ranjini and I… we've been broken for years. She doesn't want me—she hasn't touched me in months. We don't make love anymore; we barely even talk. I feel like I'm drowning, Mira. And you… you're the only one who sees me. The only one who makes me feel like I matter."

He pulled her closer, his hands trembling as they gripped her arms. Mira could see the anguish in his eyes, the deep, hollow loneliness that had driven him to this moment. She wanted to comfort him, to soothe the pain she could feel radiating from him, but she knew the line they were treading was thin and dangerous.

"Suraj, please," she said, her voice barely a whisper. "You're hurting. I understand that. But this isn't the answer.

And then out of nowhere he pulled her into his arms, burying his face in her neck. His sobs wracked his body, and Mira felt her own tears spill over as she held him, stroking his hair. He looked up at her, his face inches from hers, and in that moment, there was no mistaking the desire in his eyes.

"Mira," he whispered, his voice raw with longing. "Please. Just this once. I need to feel something real. I need to feel you."

Mira's breath hitched, a wave of conflicting emotions crashing over her. She felt the intensity of his need, the depth of his brokenness, and for a split second, she considered it. But then the clarity of her own intuition cut through the fog of the moment.

"No," she said firmly, pulling back. "Suraj, I can't. I won't. This isn't love—this is pain talking. And if we do this, we'll both regret it. You know that." He slumped against her, defeated, his body trembling.

Mira kissed his forehead gently, her tears mingling with his. "You need to forgive yourself, too. And you need to face the truth, Suraj. It's time to stop running."

She knew he had reached a breaking point, a place from which there was no turning back. Suraj stood up and started going towards the door. Mira was looking at him, she gave him a painful smile and started crying again. She could see his broken soul. Suraj turned back and hugged her tightly. He was not liking the situation in which he had put her into. He held her face with his big, strong palms and gave her a pack on her right cheek, then left cheek, then a gentle kiss on forehead, then just brushing his lips on the tip of her nose and he hesitated for a few seconds. Looked in her eyes as if pleading. Mira softly closed her eyes, feeling weak and unable to bear his looks in his eyes, she just leaned on him, her head on his big- beautiful, carved chest. Now this was the tipping point for his restraints.

He could not keep this storm inside any longer. Lifted her and took her near the big open window of the room, a cool ocean breeze was flowing. He pinned her to the side frame of the window, made her sit on the panel and held her thighs with both hands, opened them slightly, stood in between, lifted her chin and slid his tongue in her softly open mouth. Mira was in a trance-like condition. Not knowing what exactly happened, she tried to stop him by pushing him but her strength was not enough in front of his brutal, raw force. His hands were all over her as want to know her fully and this is the first opportunity in years he got. Mira was continuously crying and sighs of fear, guilt, confusion are leaving her lungs now and then. Suraj untied her night dress in a flick and let it drop down till her waist. Her beautiful, round breasts were so tender and inviting. Suraj started caressing them with admiration first then a great hunger arose and his mouth was on pink mesmerizing circles. His mouth started nibbling and then sucking those divine nipples one by one. Then in a moment he swiftly lifted her, put her on the couch and continued his search for other divine places in her body. His arms kept her down.

His hands reached her hips, he started stroking them, caressing them. Now his mouth was on the slit between her thighs. His tongue licking and sucking the nectar which laid in between those well-rounded thighs. His tongue ventured deeper and deeper into that forbidden territory. Mira wanted to stop him but could not. She is shivering, feeling chills, gasping for air. Her meek but persistent protests were not heard. She could feel his hardness on her crouch when he laid down on her and restarted kissing her face fervently, begging her to let him in. She kept crying. He unclothed himself and made place in between her legs. She tried to close her legs tightly but Suraj was not ready to take any rejection. He kept going, and at last reached where he intended to. With a few pushes he was inside her. A scream left her throat. He started moving in and out, going deeper and deeper, wanting to forget everything and just be in the moment. It kept going for some time and then Mira stopped protesting and completely surrendered to his will. 'O my, your insides are so warm and tight. I wish I had done it earlier." thoughts circling his mind. "I love you Mira, please love me back. I need you, I always needed you." He was vocal about his desire. His eyes wet with tears, body with sweat. Mira looked at him with her half-opened eyes, and slowly went into unconsciousness, a very dark place, her thoughts wavering. *Why is this happening?*

Once he reached his peak, he let out a grunting sound and came inside her. Few moments later, he called her name " Hey! Mira, Mira, open your eyes," scared, he shook her, "shit, what have I done." Reality started sinking in and he immediately realized that he did something unforgiven, very dark. Mira came to senses and started shaking due to the cold and whatever happened in the past hour. She could gather all courage at last and ask him to leave her alone.

Suraj stepped away, his face twisted in a cocktail of worry, helplessness, shame, and an unspoken promise. "I'll be back in the morning," he whispered, as if he had any say in it. He knew she needed space, yet his reluctance was palpable. Mira didn't respond. Her eyes, glassy and distant, didn't quite meet his. He left and the door shut behind him, muffling the echoes of his retreating footsteps.

Silence engulfed the room. Heavy. Unforgiving.

Mira collapsed back onto the couch, her limbs splayed out like a broken doll. Her body was a map of bruises and aches, every inch pulsating with the residual force of Suraj's desperate grip. She could still feel his fingers digging into her flesh. Her skin throbbed, but the pain was nothing compared to the turmoil inside her.

She closed her eyes, wishing for darkness but finding no solace there either. Instead, her consciousness began to drift, unmoored and untethered, floating into places she couldn't control. It was as if she were standing on the edge of a cliff, staring into a void that beckoned her with its emptiness, with the promise of release.

Her spirit wandered—into dimly lit corridors of her memory, into forgotten dreams and half-buried fears. She could feel herself leaving her body behind, lifeless on the couch, a mere shell of who she used to be. Here, in this twilight between worlds, she was weightless, but the freedom felt hollow.

A wave of cold clarity washed over her. She needed to leave. Now.

Mira struggled to her feet, her legs trembling beneath her like they were made of water. She packed and grabbed her bag, the mere act feeling monumental, as though it weighed the same as her anguish. Without another glance around, she stumbled to the door, flung it open, and stepped into the night.

The city outside was indifferent, its usual noise drowned out by the storm brewing inside her head. Mira hailed a taxi, her voice a cracked whisper, barely audible. She slid into the backseat.

The driver threw her a concerned glance in the rearview mirror, but she didn't meet his eyes. Her own were fixed on the blur of lights streaking past the window. She could feel her throat tightening, the tears threatening to spill, and she pressed her palm against her mouth to stifle a sob.

But once they started, there was no stopping them.

Her tears flowed like a river finally breaking its dam, hot and relentless. They carried with them the weight of a hundred unspoken fears, the guilt that clung to her like a second skin, the sharp sting of Suraj's pleading eyes, the phantom ache of his grip on her body. She had felt like a bird trapped in a cage, frantically beating her wings against bars she couldn't see.

Each tear was a release, but it wasn't enough. Her chest felt tight, her breaths shallow and rapid as if the air itself was a burden she couldn't bear. The sobs wracked her body, her shoulders shaking uncontrollably, but she kept her gaze fixed out the window, staring into the night as if it held answers.

Fear clung to her skin like sweat, a deep-seated terror that she couldn't quite name. It was the fear, the anxiety of having nowhere left to run.

And then there was the shame, twisting inside her like a knife for the compromises she allowed. The ghost of Suraj's touch lingered, a cruel reminder of how far she had let things spiral.

The taxi sped through the city, and Mira felt the distance grow between her and the place she had just fled from, but it wasn't far enough. She wasn't sure any distance would be far enough. Her home felt like a distant sanctuary now, a place she both longed for and dreaded, because she knew that once she was there, she would have to face herself.

Her hands were shaking as she wiped away her tears, leaving smudged trails across her cheeks. The city lights outside blurred together, like the fragments of her broken self . Her breath hitched in her throat as she tried to compose herself, but her heart raced on, untamed and wild, beating against her ribs as if it wanted to escape too.

The driver cleared his throat softly, a wordless inquiry. Mira managed a nod, indicating she was okay, or at least she would be. The words caught in her throat, and she swallowed hard, pushing down the lump that refused to go away.

As the taxi neared her home, a familiar street she once found comfort in, Mira realized she had been holding her breath. She exhaled, long and deep, as if letting go of a part of the storm that had been swirling inside her.

The car slowed to a stop, and Mira handed the driver a crumpled bill, mumbling a thanks that barely reached her own ears. She stepped out onto the pavement, the cold night air biting into her wet cheeks, grounding her back into her body, into reality. She looked up at her house, a place she had called home for years, and felt a strange disconnection, as if she were a stranger here now.

She finally entered her home. The silence hit her like a physical blow. She locked the door behind her, with a sense of finality.

Inside, she sank to the floor, curling into herself like a child. Her sobs came in waves now, quieter but deeper, pulling her under. The room felt too small, too tight. She couldn't breathe, couldn't think. It was as if the walls were closing in, pressing her into the ground, suffocating her with their silence.

For a long time, she stayed like that, clutching her knees to her chest, letting the tears flow until she felt hollowed out, until the storm inside her had spent itself.

And then there was nothing. Just the faint hum of the city outside and her own ragged breathing. She wiped her face with the back of her hand, feeling the rawness of her skin, the sting of salt against her lips.

She knew she had to get up, to keep moving, to figure out what came next. But for now, she allowed herself this one moment of stillness, this small space to grieve for the version of herself she had lost tonight, the parts she had shed to find her way back home.

Mira took a deep breath, filling her lungs with the cold, empty air of her house. Her body still ached, and her mind was a jumble of broken thoughts. But beneath it all, a tiny ember of resolve began to glow, small but steady.

She was alone now. Truly alone.

And maybe that was exactly what she needed.

Days passed by and on a crisp evening, Mira found herself on the terrace, the sky above painted with hues of twilight, the sun a fading ember on the horizon. The air was cool and carried a gentle whisper, almost as if it recognized the magic she was about to invoke. She spread a blanket across the floor, the fabric soft and familiar beneath her fingers. Around her, laid out with reverence, were her tarot decks—each one a piece of her heart, a fragment of her soul.

The decks were a mosaic of her journey, from the first, weathered with use and love, to the newest, vibrant and unblemished. Mira's fingers traced the edges of her favourite one, the one she had created herself. It was special, not just because of its art but because of the essence it carried—her essence. She had spent countless hours sketching, conceptualizing, and breathing life into these cards. Every line, every colour, every symbol was deliberate, a manifestation of her vision, her connection to the unseen.

She remembered the process vividly—how she had envisioned the themes, drawn rough sketches late into the night, and meticulously painted each card with care. Her fingertips still remembered the feel of the brush, the stroke of ink across the canvas. It was more than just art; it was a labour of love, a sacred act of creation. These cards were not simply tools—they were portals, holding the whispers of the universe, the voices only she could hear.

Mira picked up one of her own creations, a card she called The Whisperer. The illustration was intricate, the figure in the card poised as if listening intently to the winds of time. She smiled, a sense of pride welling up inside her. This deck, her masterpiece, held a special place in her heart. It was born from a deep part of her psyche, an expression of her innermost knowing, and the bond she shared with it was profound, almost maternal.

Tonight, under the open sky, Mira felt a deep resonance with her cards, a connection that went beyond their physical form. She shuffled them gently, feeling the smooth glide of the cards between her fingers. It was as if she were touching a part of herself, the part that existed in a space beyond words, beyond time. She drew a deep breath, inhaling the cool night air, and let herself sink into the moment.

These decks were her companions, her guides, and her teachers. They had seen her through sleepless nights, moments of uncertainty, and waves of intuition that had led her to profound realizations. Each reading was a dance between the cards and her consciousness, an intimate exchange where she allowed the universe to speak through her creations.

As she drew her first card, the breeze picked up slightly, rustling the leaves and carrying the scent of blooming jasmine. Mira felt the familiar tingle at the back of her neck, the signal that something—or someone—was listening. She looked down at the card in her hand and smiled. Tonight, her decks were ready to reveal their secrets, and she was ready to listen.

Suraj's calls came like a relentless tide, each one tugging at Mira, trying to pull her back into waters she was no longer willing to wade into. Her phone vibrated on the coffee table, his name flashing on the screen for the fifth time that hour. Mira glanced at it, her fingers hovering over the screen before she turned away, pressing her lips into a thin line. She wasn't ready—not now, maybe not ever. Her heart was still bruised from their last encounter, the intensity of it, the force, the chaos he brought into her carefully rebuilt world.

She knew what he wanted. An apology? Closure? A chance to explain himself? Declaration of love? But Mira couldn't give him that, not now when the echo of his grip still ached in her bones, when the memory of his desperate eyes still haunted her. It wasn't just the physical pain; it was the weight of the emotional storm he had hurled at her, the raw, unfiltered desperation she wasn't prepared for.

Mira picked up her phone and silenced it, letting it fall back onto the table like a stone sinking into deep waters. She closed her eyes, willing herself to breathe, to focus on the present moment, the sanctuary she had created for herself. She knew she was avoiding him, dodging the confrontation she knew was inevitable. But she also knew her boundaries now, knew the importance of honouring her own space, her own healing. It wasn't about fear—it was about self-preservation.

In the midst of it all, there was Ranjini.

Ranjini had called her yesterday, her voice lighter, softer, carrying a melody that Mira hadn't heard in a long time. They spoke easily, as good friends. Mira listened as Ranjini spoke about her new projects, her plans for a quiet trip to the mountains, the newfound joy she was discovering in her solitude. There was a calmness in her voice, a sense of peace that Mira had hoped she would find.

"Suraj and I," Ranjini had said with a gentle sigh, "we needed different things. It took me a while, but I see it clearly now. There's no anger left, Mira. I only wish him well." The words were genuine, without the jagged edges of resentment. Ranjini had found her own closure, her own freedom from the tangled web they had all once been caught in.

Mira hadn't told Ranjini about what happened between her and Suraj—about that last, disastrous encounter. She didn't want to taint Ranjini's healing with the darkness of her own recent past. It was her burden to bear, her story to process. Instead, she listened, a soft smile playing on her lips, feeling relief wash over her. Knowing that Ranjini had moved on without bitterness filled her with a quiet kind of happiness.

It was strange how life had twisted their paths, how the connections between them had frayed and mended in unexpected ways. Mira felt no jealousy, no discomfort in hearing Ranjini's contentment. Instead, she felt a warmth, a silent acknowledgment of a chapter that had closed for good. Ranjini had made peace with it. Perhaps, someday, she would too.

But for now, Mira needed the distance, the silence. She needed to feel the quiet strength she was slowly reclaiming. She wasn't ready to face Suraj's questions, his pleas, his apologies. Not until she was sure of herself again, sure that she wouldn't be pulled back into the chaos she had fought so hard to escape.

She picked up her deck of cards, her fingers tracing the familiar lines of The Whisperer. She shuffled them slowly, allowing the rhythm to ground her, to remind her of the journey she was on— one that didn't involve him anymore.

Chapter 22

Atmaj had been away from the city for several weeks, his absence creating a void Mira could not quite fill despite her daily meditation, writing, and deep conversations with herself. He had gone to Europe to participate in a full marathon—a challenge he had been training for relentlessly over the past year. It wasn't just a race for him; it was a pilgrimage of sorts, a way to test his physical limits, confront his inner demons, and discover new aspects of himself.

The marathon was set in the scenic region of Provence, France, where winding roads stretched through lavender fields and vineyards, against a backdrop of historic chateaus and rolling hills. He had told Mira before leaving, his eyes sparkling with anticipation, "This isn't just a race. It's a journey I need to take—for myself, and maybe, for us too."

He left with a small group of close friends, fellow runners who shared his passion for endurance sports. The trip became an adventure of its own. He called Mira from Paris, a few days before the marathon, describing how he felt standing at the Eiffel Tower, the crisp autumn air filling his lungs. He sent her photos of cobblestone streets, quaint cafes, and the sunset over the Seine. "I wish you were here," he texted her, followed by a picture of the moonlight dancing on the river's surface.

On the day of the marathon, the weather was perfect—a mild chill in the air, with a clear blue sky overhead. The race was gruelling, stretching across 42 kilometres of varied terrain. Atmaj could feel the adrenaline pumping through his veins as he started, the sound of hundreds of running shoes hitting the ground like a heartbeat of a giant, unified body.

He told Mira later that the first half of the race felt like a dream, the beauty of the landscape keeping his spirits high. He ran past rows of sunflowers, waving at cheering locals who handed out oranges and water. He caught sight of a little girl holding a sign that read, "You are stronger than you think," and it made him smile, thinking of Mira's words to him before he left: You can do this. You have the strength of the mountains within you.

But the real test came in the second half. At the 30-kilometer mark, exhaustion hit him like a wave. His legs felt like lead, every step heavier than the last. He pushed through the pain, drawing strength from the thought of Mira waiting for him, picturing her proud smile when he would share the news of his finish. He whispered her name like a mantra, letting it pull him forward.

When he crossed the finish line, tears welled up in his eyes. He had done it. He had faced his limits and conquered them. He texted Mira right away: "I made it. I finished." There was a photo too, of him holding his medal, his face flushed but glowing with triumph. Mira's heart soared with pride when she received it, and she could almost feel his heartbeat in sync with her own, despite the distance.

After the marathon, Atmaj spent a few more days exploring the French countryside, visiting local vineyards, tasting wine, and immersing himself in the culture. He shared little anecdotes with Mira—how he met an old French runner who had completed the marathon every year for the past three decades, how he got lost in a small village and ended up having dinner with a local family who treated him like their own.

He called her from a quiet spot by the Rhône River, the sound of water flowing softly in the background. "I feel like I've found a part of myself here," he told her. "It's strange, but being away has made me realize how much I need to be close to you, Mira. I can't wait to come back."

The day he returned, he messaged her: I'm back in the city. When can I see you? She had been waiting for this message for days, her heart aching with the longing she had suppressed while he was away.

"Come over," she replied simply. There was no need for grand gestures or elaborate plans. They both knew the place they felt the most at home was in each other's presence.

When he arrived at her place, she opened the door and for a moment, neither of them said a word. They just stood there, looking at each other, absorbing the moment. He looked tanned, a little leaner, and his eyes held a new depth, as if he had carried back a piece of the French landscape within them. She reached out and touched his face gently, as if to make sure he was real.

"You did it," she whispered, her voice filled with emotion. He nodded, pulling her into a tight embrace. "I did it. But I missed you more than I can put into words."

They spent the evening talking, curled up on her couch with cups of tea. He shared every detail—how he felt during the race, the people he met, the sights he saw. Mira listened intently, smiling and laughing, but there was a hint of something he couldn't quite place in her eyes. He asked her a few times if she was alright, sensing that something was off, but she brushed it off with a reassuring smile.

Later that night, they took their blankets and pillows up to the terrace, deciding to sleep under the stars. The night sky was clear, a canvas of deep blue dotted with silver stars, and the air carried the faint scent of blooming jasmine.

Atmaj lay beside Mira, propped up on one elbow, looking down at her face. He could see the shadows of her unspoken worries and wanted nothing more than to kiss them away. He began massaging her shoulders, feeling the knots of tension beneath his fingers. His touch was gentle, tender, and she melted under his hands, letting out a small sigh.

"You've been carrying too much," he said softly, pressing a kiss to her forehead. "Let me take some of it away." His hands moved slowly, massaging her back, her neck, tracing the curve of her spine. He kissed her softly, again and again, as if trying to convey all the love and longing he had felt in their weeks apart.

Mira felt a surge of love, a warmth that spread from her chest to the tips of her fingers and toes. It was like a wave, crashing over her, sweeping away her fears, her loneliness. She looked up at him, her eyes brimming with unshed tears. "I love you," she said, her voice a whisper carried away by the breeze.

He leaned down, capturing her lips in a deep, slow kiss, his hands cradling her face as if she were something fragile and precious. "I love you too, Mira," he murmured against her lips. They lay there together, wrapped in each other, the stars above them witnessing their silent vows, their unspoken promises. And for that night, at least, everything felt perfect again.

Chapter 23

Mira and Atmaj receive a special, private invitation to a tea ceremony hosted by Saraswati, a close friend and spiritual mentor who lives in the serene outskirts of the Western Ghats. Saraswati's home, nestled within dense foliage and abundant with the scent of blooming wildflowers, feels like a sanctuary. This invitation is unique because it is not just a social event; it is a spiritual experience, guided by a French man named Lucien from the Auroville community. Lucien, an ascetic figure with gentle eyes and an aura of calm, has devoted his life to spiritual practices and rituals from various cultures, including the traditional tea ceremony.

The tea ceremony Lucien conducts is not simply a matter of tasting tea. It is a mindful, meditative practice rooted in ancient traditions, primarily inspired by the Zen Buddhist culture of Japan, though it has deep connections with Chinese and Korean practices as well. Lucien's adaptation has a unique blend, influenced by his spiritual journey in Auroville, where he connected deeply with nature, simplicity, and the present moment.

The tea ceremony is an act of devotion, designed to cultivate mindfulness, gratitude, and inner peace. It's a celebration of simplicity, the beauty of nature, and the transient moments of life. It symbolizes the impermanence of existence and the importance of being fully present. For Lucien, it is a way to connect with his guests on a deeper, soulful level, allowing them to experience a shared silence, a space of reflection, and a bond beyond words.

The ceremony is held in Saraswati's garden, a place filled with the soft hum of bees and the rustling of leaves. A gentle breeze carries the earthy fragrance of the surrounding forest. Lucien has prepared a space with meticulous care: a low wooden table sits atop a woven mat, surrounded by cushions for comfortable seating. The table is adorned with simple yet elegant elements – a handmade tea set, an incense burner emitting a thin trail of sandalwood smoke, and a small vase with a single lotus flower, symbolizing purity and enlightenment.

Mira and Atmaj arrive, dressed in light, comfortable clothing. Saraswati welcomes them warmly and introduces them to Lucien. They exchange pleasantries, but there is a hushed reverence in the air, an unspoken understanding that this moment holds a deeper

Lucien bows deeply to his guests before taking his place at the head of the table. He begins by explaining the philosophy behind the tea ceremony, speaking in soft, measured tones.

"The tea ceremony is not about the tea itself," Lucien says, looking into the eyes of Mira and Atmaj with a serene smile. "It is about the shared presence, the simplicity of this moment. It is a way to honour the earth, the water, the fire, and the air that have brought us this humble drink. It is about finding the divine in the mundane."

He lights a candle and bows once more, signalling the start of the ritual. The guests remain silent, observing the delicate yet deliberate movements of Lucien as he prepares the tea. Every action is precise, almost like a dance. He rinses the tea cups with hot water, wipes them dry with a soft cloth, and places them gently in front of each guest.

The tea he uses is a blend of delicate, handpicked leaves from the Auroville community's tea garden, infused with herbs and flowers known for their calming and grounding properties. The aroma is floral and earthy, evoking a sense of calm even before the first sip.

Lucien serves the tea with a graceful bow. He invites everyone to hold their cups, feel the warmth in their hands, and inhale the fragrant steam. He encourages them to take a moment of silence, to express gratitude inwardly for the elements and beings that contributed to this simple cup of tea.

Mira closes her eyes, feeling a sense of grounding and connection. The warm ceramic cup in her hands feels like a link to the earth itself. She breathes in the aroma, which seems to open a doorway to memories she cannot place, a deep sense of nostalgia for something timeless. When she takes the first sip, the tea feels like liquid tranquillity, its warmth spreading through her chest and calming her mind.

Atmaj, on the other hand, finds himself observing the entire process with a childlike curiosity. He has always been fascinated by rituals, but this one feels different. It is not filled with chanting or elaborate gestures; it is simple, almost ordinary. Yet, in its simplicity, he feels a profound depth. As he drinks the tea, he feels a wave of relaxation wash over him, as though he is shedding layers of accumulated stress and thoughts.

The silence between sips is thick with unspoken understanding. Mira and Atmaj exchange a glance, and for a moment, they are not in a garden with friends; they are in a shared mental space, a void where words are unnecessary, where only the purity of the moment exists.

After the tea is finished, Lucien speaks softly again, inviting everyone to share their feelings if they wish. Saraswati goes first, expressing her gratitude for the presence of her friends and the opportunity to share such a sacred moment. Her eyes are bright with unshed tears, a sign of the profound peace she feels.

Mira, still holding the empty cup, looks at Lucien and then at the lotus flower on the table. "It felt like time stopped," she says slowly, her voice tinged with awe. "I could feel every part of the process – the earth, the water, the fire – as if the whole universe had condensed into this single cup of tea."

Atmaj nods in agreement, his usually expressive face unusually calm. "I've never felt so present," he admits. "I thought I knew mindfulness, but this... this was different. It was like being a part of something eternal."

Lucien bows his head, a smile of contentment playing on his lips. "The tea ceremony," he says, "is a reminder that the divine can be found in the simplest of actions, if only we take the time to look."

As they rise from their seats, the sun is beginning its descent, casting a golden light over the garden. Mira feels lighter, as though a heavy burden she didn't know she was carrying has been lifted. She takes Atmaj's hand, and they exchange a silent promise – to bring this sense of mindfulness, this peace, into their everyday lives.

On the drive back home, they remain quiet, each lost in their own reflections. The experience has touched something deep within them, something beyond words, leaving a lasting impression that they will carry with them, a quiet reminder of the power of presence, simplicity, gratitude and the sacredness of everyday rituals.

Chapter 24

Mira sat in her cozy corner with a steaming cup of tea when her phone pinged with a message from Ranjini, an old friend. The message was unusually long, and Mira's heart warmed as she opened it.

> "Dearest Mira,

I hope this message finds you well and immersed in your magical world as always. I have news that I've been eager to share with you—I'm getting married again! Life has given me another chance at happiness, and I've decided to grab it with both hands. I'm writing to you not just as a friend, but as someone whose presence in my life has been a gift.

The wedding will be an intimate affair, a destination celebration in the enchanting backwaters of Kerala, amidst temples, lush greenery, and the sounds of ancient rituals. I would be honoured if you could join me with a plus one. Bring someone who holds a special place in your heart.

It would mean the world to me if you could be there. We'll have the Mehendi, the Sangeet, the wedding ceremony at a traditional temple, and a final reception by the beach. I'm looking forward to dancing with you under the stars.

With love,

Ranjini."

Chapter 25

Mira's face broke into a soft smile, but the thought of a plus one made her pause. Her heart instinctively reached for Atmaj. She picked up her phone and dialled his number.

Mira Invites Atmaj:

"Hey, I just got a wedding invitation," Mira started, her voice laced with a tinge of excitement.

Atmaj's voice softened on the other end. "Sounds like a beautiful affair. Who's getting married?"

"Ranjini. She's remarrying and wants me to bring a plus one. Would you be my plus one, Atmaj?"

There was a moment of silence before Atmaj responded, his tone filled with affection. "Mira, I'd go anywhere with you, even if it were a trip to the underworld. Of course, I'll come."

Mira's laughter was light, but a flicker of anxiety crossed her face. She hadn't mentioned the part about Suraj being there. The shadow of the past lurked in her mind, and she pushed it aside, determined not to let it cloud her moment with Atmaj.

The Destination Wedding:

The destination was nothing short of a dream—Kerala's backwaters, framed by swaying coconut trees, serene lakes, and the smell of the sea mingling with the heady aroma of incense.

The temple where the ceremony was to be held stood tall, its intricately carved pillars whispering stories of devotion and time.

The festivities began with the Mehendi. Mira and Atmaj found themselves surrounded by laughter, music, and women with hands stained in deep hues of henna. Mira's own hands bore delicate designs.

It was during the Sangeet that she saw Suraj. He stood across the room, dressed in a simple yet elegant kurta, his gaze fixed on her with an intensity that made her breath catch. Memories she had tried to bury surfaced, leaving her feeling raw and exposed. The night at his place, his advances, the betrayal—it all came rushing back, overwhelming her. She excused herself and hurried out into the gardens, needing space to breathe.

But Suraj followed. He was relentless.

"Mira, wait!" His voice was a sharp whisper, filled with an urgency she hadn't heard before. He caught up to her, grabbing her arm gently but firmly.

"Let go of me," Mira hissed, her eyes glistening with unshed tears. Her anxiety bubbled over, and she felt her chest tightening, as if the walls of the world were closing in.

 Suraj pleaded, his voice breaking. "I can't live without you, Mira. I made a mistake—a terrible mistake, I know."

Mira's resolve shattered, and she broke down, the sobs wracking her body as she tried to push him away. "You had no right! You violated everything I trusted, everything I thought was sacred between us. How dare you confess your love to me? "

His hands on her arms, the intensity of his plea, it was too much. She felt trapped, cornered by his love and his guilt. Her anxiety morphed into panic, her breaths coming in short gasps. She tried to step back, but he wouldn't let go.

As Suraj knelt in the moonlit garden, pleading with Mira, fragments of their shared past flooded his mind. He could almost see her as she once was—the bright, spirited girl from college who had captivated him from the very first day.

Suraj remembered the first time he saw Mira in their college library. She was engrossed in a thick book, her hair pulled back into a messy bun, a faint smile playing on her lips as she turned a page. There was a quiet elegance about her, an ethereal quality that made her seem like she belonged to a different world. He had sat a few tables away, pretending to read while stealing glances at her, afraid that if he looked too long, the spell she cast would break.

They became friends after that, almost accidentally. He had found her struggling with a stack of books, and without thinking, he had reached out to help her. The smile she gave him then, so genuine and warm, had been the moment he felt his heart slip out of his control.

"You're always reading," he had teased her once, sitting across from her at the college canteen. "Do you ever put those books down and see the real world?"

Mira had laughed, that musical sound that still echoed in his memories. "Maybe I see the world more clearly through these stories than others do with their own eyes," she had replied, her gaze meeting him with a spark of something he couldn't quite place then.

It was in those quiet, shared moments that Suraj realized he loved her. Not just admired or respected her, but loved her with a depth that terrified him. He never told her, not outright. He was content to be her friend, to listen to her dreams, to share in her laughter. He had thought that just being near her was enough.

But over time, the quiet admiration grew into something more, something fierce and all-consuming. He started wanting more from her—more time, more attention, more of her heart. It gnawed at him when she'd mention other men she was interested in, even though he hid his jealousy behind a mask of indifference. He was always there for her, the loyal friend, but inside, he was fighting a losing battle against his own desires.

"You don't understand, Mira. We're meant to be together. I know you feel it too."

"Stop, Suraj," she had pleaded, trying to push him away. "You're scaring me. Please, let me go."

"Don't," she had cut him off, her voice choking with tears. "Don't say anything. You've ruined everything, Suraj.

"Please, Mira," he whispered, his voice raw with emotion. "I've carried this regret every single day since that night. I was selfish, I was wrong. I thought if I pushed hard enough, you'd see how much I loved you. I didn't realize I was only pushing you away."

Mira's eyes were filled with tears, her face a mask of pain and anger. "You broke me that night, Suraj. You shattered the trust I had in you, and you left me to pick up the pieces alone. You say you loved me, but love doesn't hurt like that."

Suraj's voice broke as he spoke, his tears mingling with the raindrops that had begun to fall. "I've changed, Mira. I've learned from my mistakes. Please, give me a chance to show you I can be the man you deserve."

Mira, her voice was trembling, asked, "If you loved me for so long, why didn't you ever tell me before, Suraj? Not in college, not afterwards… Why now?" Her eyes brim with unshed tears, filled with anguish and disbelief. "You never gave me any hint that you had these feelings for me. You never let me in… So why now, when it's too late?"

Suraj, overwhelmed by the rawness of her pain, kneeled before her, his head bowed. He takes a deep breath, struggling to find the right words. "Mira, I couldn't tell you… I wasn't brave enough then. I thought you deserved better. I wasn't ready to face my own demons, and by the time I realized what I had lost, you were already gone… living your life, moving on. I thought it was best for you."

Mira's turmoil is evident; her heart ached, a whirlwind of emotions tearing her apart. She wanted to soften, to forgive, but the memories of their last encounter, the hurt and betrayal she felt, refuse to let go. Her face hardened, and she stepped back, trying to distance herself from the pull she felt towards him.

Suraj, with desperation in his eyes, stood up from his kneeling position. He opened his arms wide, a gesture of complete surrender. "Mira, I'm here now. I'm not hiding anymore. I'm begging you... Give me one chance to make things right."

Mira's resolve crumbled, her legs gave away, and she collapsed into his arms, unconscious. Suraj caught her swiftly, panic flashing in his eyes. Without a second thought, he carried her to his hotel, just a short walk away from the wedding venue.

Mira laid on the bed, still unconscious but breathing steadily. The room was dimly lit, casting long shadows that flicker across the walls. Suraj sat beside her, his face etched with sorrow and regret. He took her hand, holding it gently, almost afraid she might pull away even in her sleep.

He began to speak, his voice low, almost a whisper. "I don't know if you can hear me, Mira... but I need to tell you everything now, while I still can." His words tremble with raw honesty. "My life has been a mess since I let you go. I made choices I can't undo. I thought I was protecting you by staying away, but I was just a coward."

He paused , swallowing hard as tears welled up. "Ranjini... I thought she was the answer to my loneliness. But it became a toxic cycle. I was trapped. And then... my business partner... he was murdered, and they suspect me. I've been questioned endlessly. My own mother has cancer now. I'm watching her fade away, and there's no one by my side. I tried to end it all once... I thought it would be better that way."

Suraj's voice broke and he pressed Mira's hand to his forehead, a gesture of surrender. "I don't expect you to love me, Mira. I don't deserve it. But I just needed you to know... you were always the one. You were my light, and I lost it."

To his surprise, Mira's fingers curled slightly around his hand. He looked up, and her eyes were open, glistening with tears. She pulled herself up and, without a word, wrapped her arms around him, holding him close.

For a moment, they simply stayed like that, two souls embracing the comfort they had long denied themselves. Mira's voice was barely above a whisper as she admitted, "I wanted you too, Suraj. I did... back in those days. But you never gave me a reason to believe it. I thought I had to move on. I thought you didn't care."

Suraj tightened his hold, burying his face in her shoulder, his own tears falling freely now. "I was a fool, Mira. I thought you never loved me more than a good friend. I was so afraid of losing you that I lost you anyway."

Mira gently pulled back to look into his eyes, her hand cupping his face. "I can't forget what happened, Suraj. I can't just erase the pain. But I'm here now, and so are you. Maybe that's all we have for tonight."

Suraj nodded, his gaze locked with hers, a silent understanding passing between them. They might not have all the answers, but for now, they had each other, and that is enough.

Chapter 26

Atmaj was sitting by the window, the soft glow of the city lights was casting shadows across his face. His eyes were distant, filled with worry, searching for answers he didn't have. He had been looking for Mira for hours, his heart was pounding with anxiety, yet when he called her, her voice was calm, almost detached. She told him she was on her way back.

The door creaked open, and Mira steps inside, looking exhausted, like she's been carrying a heavy burden. Atmaj rose to his feet immediately, his expression a mix of relief and concern. He crossed the room in a few quick strides and gently took her hands in his.

"Mira, where were you? I've been looking everywhere," he says softly, his voice tinged with fear he rarely shows.

Mira took a deep breath, avoiding his eyes for a moment. "I'm fine sweetheart. I... I needed some time." Her voice trembles slightly.

"Take your time," he says quietly, a promise in his voice that he's here, no matter what she's about to say.

Mira closed her eyes for a moment, steadying herself. "It's about Suraj. He... he confessed many things tonight," she began, her words coming out slowly, as if each one carries the weight of the past. He told me he's loved me for years passionately, even back in college, but he never said a word in fear of losing. Not until tonight."

Atmaj's face was unreadable, but his grip on her hands tightened just slightly. He doesn't interrupt; he knows she needs to get it all out.

"I never told you why I had to come back in a hurry from Kundapura. You were busy with your France trip. I didn't want to talk about it to anyone."

Atmaj's eyes flashed with a momentary flicker of something she had never seen before but he still said nothing, holding space for her.

"Today he poured his heart out. He spoke about his life, his struggles, his regrets. He's been through so much, Atmaj. He even... he even tried to end his own life once," Mira's voice drops to a whisper, tears streaming down her face now.

Atmaj wiped a tear away from her cheek gently, his own expression softening. "Mira..." he begins, but she shakes her head, needing to finish.

"I hugged him, Atmaj. I couldn't help it. At that moment, I felt... something. I don't know if it was love or pity or just a memory of what might have been. But I held him, and I told him that once, a long time ago, I did have feelings for him too. I never said it out loud before tonight."

The silence that followed was thick and heavy, filled with everything left unsaid. Mira finally looked up at him, searching his face for a reaction, terrified of what she might find.

"Say something," she whispers. "I don't know what you're thinking."

Atmaj let out a long, slow breath, closing his eyes briefly as if trying to gather his own thoughts. When he opened them, they were filled with a tenderness she didn't expect.

"You told me everything, Mira," he says softly. "You didn't have to, but you did. And that means more to me than you can imagine."

He took her face in his hands, forced her to look directly at him. "I've known you long enough to understand your heart. I can't say it doesn't hurt to hear all of this, because it does. But what matters is that you chose to come back to me tonight. You chose to tell me the truth."

Mira's lip quivers, and she tries to look away, but he won't let her. "I don't know how you can be so calm about this," she admits. "I thought you'd be hurt, or... I don't know...."

Atmaj's eyes softened further, and he pulled her into his arms, holding her tightly. "Mira, I've seen the way you look at me, the way you chose me, again and again. I trust you. I trust us. Whatever happened tonight, whatever you felt for Suraj... it's a part of your story. But it's not our story."

He pulled back slightly, tilting her chin up so she would look directly into his eyes. "I won't pretend this doesn't sting. It does. But I love you, Mira. And I'm here. I'm not going anywhere."

Mira broke down then, sobbing into his chest, the release of emotions she didn't realize she'd been holding back. Atmaj held her, stroking her hair, whispering soothing words.

Mira leaned in, pressing her forehead to his, taking a deep, shuddering breath. "Thank you," she whispered. "For loving me, even when I'm a mess."

He just smiled and then reminded her that she was saying something about Kundapura. Mira stiffened, her eyes darting away from him. She swallowed hard, trying to come up with an answer, but words seemed to escape her. "It's nothing," she muttered, her voice barely a whisper. "Will tell you some other time."

Atmaj's gaze softened, but there was a hint of determination in his eyes. He reached out, taking her trembling hands in his, holding them gently. "No, Mira. It's not 'nothing.' I can feel it. Ever since I came back from France, you've been different. But distant. There's something you're not telling me, and I need to know what it is."

Mira's heart pounded in her chest, a wave of fear and shame washing over her. She bit her lip, shaking her head, trying to pull her hands away, but Atmaj didn't let go. He tightened his grip slightly, not in force, but in reassurance.

"Talk to me," he pleaded softly. "Whatever it is, I want to hear it. I'm here, Mira."

Mira finally looked at him, her face a mask of sorrow. "You may hate me," she whispered. "You'll never look at me the same way again."

Atmaj got worried but pulled her closer to him and squeezed her tight. "It's your wish Mira if you don't want to speak now about that incident." As soon as Mira heard his tender words, her breathing turned heavy and ragged.

Mira took a deep breath, feeling the lump in her throat grow tighter. She felt like she was standing on the edge of a cliff, about to jump. "It's about Suraj,"

"Ok, what about him?" He asked peacefully with a wrinkled forehead. She told him what exactly happened on that dark night. She had to. This secret was becoming an open untreated wound for her soul. When Mira finally found the strength to tell Atmaj the truth about Suraj, her voice wavered, and she looked away, unable to meet his eyes. It was a moment she had dreaded— exposing the dark, vile experience she had carried like a burden in the deepest corners of her soul.

Atmaj listened, his body tense, fingers gripping the edge of his chair as if it were the only thing keeping him grounded. He could see the agony in her eyes, the haunted look that spoke of betrayal, shame, and a violation that had scarred her deeply. It wasn't just the words she was saying; it was the way she curled into herself, like she was trying to disappear. With every detail Mira shared, his heart cracked a little more. And then she spoke of the moment when Suraj forced himself on her—when her trust, her dignity, her voice had been stolen.

A visceral rage surged through Atmaj like he had never felt before. It was as if something primal and ancient had been unleashed inside him, a force of fury that clawed at his chest, demanding release. He felt his pulse racing, his breath turning ragged, the world narrowing into a tunnel of red-hot anger. The bile rose in his throat as he clenched his fists so tightly that his knuckles turned white.

"How dare he?" Atmaj's voice was low and guttural, trembling with the raw intensity of his wrath. "How dare he do this to you, and then express his feelings for you today after what he did.

Lover doesn't rape, he makes love. He doesn't force himself, he knows patience, he sacrifices."

His voice cracked, a mixture of outrage and deep, aching empathy. He reached out, cupping Mira's face gently in his hands, his thumb wiping away the tears that had begun to spill down her cheeks. He could see the pain she had carried alone for so long, the burden she had borne in silence, and it broke him. He wished he could take away every ounce of her suffering, every moment of fear she had endured.

"Mira, I am so, so sorry," he whispered, his voice hoarse, filled with a tenderness that contrasted the violent storm brewing inside him. He pulled her close, wrapping his arms around her as if he could shield her from the memory, from the hurt.

But soon tenderness got replaced by something cold, sharp, and unforgiving. He stood up abruptly, pacing the room like a caged animal.

Chapter 27

Atmaj stormed down the narrow hotel corridor, the dim lights flickering like the pulse of his rage. He didn't bother knocking. The door slammed open, hitting the wall with a dull thud. Inside, Suraj looked up from where he was sitting, his expression weary, almost expectant, as if he'd known this moment was inevitable.

Without a word, Atmaj lunged forward, grabbing Suraj by the collar and yanking him to his feet.

"You think you can just sit there, pretending everything's fine?" Atmaj hissed, his grip tightening. "Get up. Face me like a man."

Suraj rose slowly, hands at his sides, offering no resistance. His eyes held no anger—only a deep, unspoken sorrow.

"I'm not going to fight you, Atmaj," Suraj said quietly. "I deserve this. I won't stop you."

Atmaj's fist connected with Suraj's jaw, a brutal hit that sent him reeling. Suraj stumbled but didn't retaliate. Blood trickled from the corner of his mouth, but he merely wiped it away, his expression unchanged.

"You deserve more than this," Atmaj snarled, his voice trembling with the force of his emotions. "You deserve to feel the same pain you put her through. She trusted you, and you betrayed her in the worst way possible."

Suraj nodded slowly, his eyes welling up with unshed tears. "I know," he whispered. "I've been living with that guilt every day. I can't undo what I did. I lost control, and I became someone I never wanted to be."

Another punch landed, this time in Suraj's stomach, making him double over in pain. He gasped for breath but made no move to defend himself.

"You call that love?" Atmaj's voice was thick with contempt. "You hurt her, made her doubt herself, broke something inside her that may never heal. That's not love—that's possession. Obsession."

Suraj sank to the floor, his shoulders shaking, tears spilling down his cheeks. "You're right," he choked out. "I let my fear of losing her destroy everything. I was selfish. I thought I loved her, but I didn't know what love truly meant. I still care about her, but I've accepted that I lost her the moment I crossed that line."

Atmaj stepped back, his fists still clenched, but the raw pain in Suraj's voice gave him pause. He stared at the man before him, seeing not the monster he'd imagined, but a broken soul who had lost his way.

The door creaked open, and Mira stepped into the room, her face a mix of shock and sadness. She glanced from Atmaj's clenched fists to Suraj's bruised face, her eyes filling with tears.

"What are you doing?" Mira's voice was calm, but there was an edge to it, a strength that made both men fall silent. "Atmaj, stop. This isn't helping."

"Mira, he hurt you," Atmaj said, his voice strained. "He broke you. How can you ask me to stop?"

Mira stepped closer, placing a hand on Atmaj's chest, her touch gentle yet firm. "Because this won't heal anything," she said softly. "Hitting him won't erase the pain. It won't undo what's happened."

She turned to Suraj, kneeling beside him. Suraj looked up at her, his face contorted with regret, his eyes pleading for a forgiveness he wasn't sure he deserved.

"I'm sorry, Mira," Suraj whispered, his voice raw. "I've wanted nothing but to take it all back. I never meant to become this person. I never meant to hurt you."

Mira's hand gently touched his cheek, a gesture filled with a strange, bittersweet tenderness. "I know," she said. "And I forgive you—not because you deserve it, but because I need to. I can't carry this pain anymore. It's too heavy. But forgiveness doesn't mean I forget what happened, Suraj. It means I'm choosing to move forward."

Suraj nodded, a tear slipping down his face. "Thank you," he said, his voice barely a whisper. "I don't deserve your kindness, but… thank you."

Atmaj stepped forward, wrapping his arms around Mira, pulling her close. He pressed a kiss to her forehead, his eyes filled with a mix of love and appreciation.

Mira looked up at him, her expression softening. Then she turned back to Suraj, extending her hand. "Don't disappear from our lives, Suraj," she said. "I don't want you to waste your life in regret. Find your own path. Live better. For both our sakes."

Suraj took her hand, squeezing it lightly. "I promise," he said. "I'll try."

Atmaj's eyes hardened slightly as he looked at Suraj, his voice low and firm. "But know this: if you ever hurt her again—if you even come close—I won't hold back next time."

Suraj nodded, his face a picture of solemn resolve. "I understand," he said. "And I swear I'll never hurt her again."

Mira stepped back into Atmaj's arms, the tension in the room easing slightly, though something heavy lingered in the air—a sense of unfinished business, unresolved emotions that couldn't be neatly tied up.

Atmaj kissed Mira gently, as if grounding himself in her presence.

Mira looked far, her gaze distant. And she was thinking, "life is uncertain, and sometimes we don't get the answers we want. We just have to live with the questions. I don't know what the future holds for me, for Suraj."

Atmaj held her close, the silence stretching out between them, filled with things left unsaid. As they turned to leave, Suraj watched them go, a faint, bittersweet smile on his lips. He knew this was the end of one chapter, but the shadows of their shared past still lingered, casting a long, uncertain shadow over the future.

The door closed softly behind them, leaving the room empty except for the echo of unspoken words and the mystery of what might still lie ahead.

Chapter 28

The sun was setting, casting a golden hue across the room. Mira sat cross-legged on the sofa, deep in thought, while Atmaj leaned back, watching her with a gentle, curious expression.

Mira sat by the window, watching the fading light of the sunset as it painted the sky in shades of pink and gold. The phone felt cold in her hand as she dialled the familiar number. It had been a long time since she last reached out to him, and her heart fluttered with a mix of anticipation and uncertainty.

After a few rings, a calm, steady voice answered on the other end. "Mira, it's been a while. What a surprise to hear from you."

Mira felt a small, fleeting smile touch her lips, but it quickly faded. "Hi, Abhay," she said, her voice tinged with a vulnerability she hadn't expected. "Yes, it's been too long. I wish I were just calling to catch up, but... I need your help."

There was a brief silence, the kind that only existed between old friends who understood the weight behind each word. Abhay's tone softened, sensing the gravity in her voice. "Of course, Mira. You sound troubled. What's going on?"

Mira took a deep breath, her fingers tracing the patterns on the wooden table beside her. "Something happened recently," she began, her voice faltering slightly. "It was with an old friend, Suraj. It left me feeling... shattered. But it's more than that. I can't shake this feeling that the pain we've experienced isn't just from this lifetime. It feels like a thread from the past, something unresolved pulling me back."

Abhay's silence on the line spoke volumes, a thoughtful pause as he considered her words. "You've always been sensitive to these connections," he finally said, his voice gentle. "If you're feeling that pull, it's worth exploring. But Mira, you know better than anyone—you're too emotionally involved to do this on your own. It's easy to blur the lines between memory and emotion when you're this close."

Mira nodded, even though he couldn't see her. She had known this herself, but hearing it from Abhay felt like a confirmation she needed. "That's why I'm calling you," she admitted. "I need someone I trust. I need your guidance. Will you help me? Can we do a regression session?"

There was a warmth in Abhay's voice now, a reassuring calm that wrapped around her like a soft blanket. "Of course, Mira," he said without hesitation. "Let's do this tomorrow. I'll make time for you. We'll take it slowly, uncover whatever needs to be seen, and I'll be with you every step of the way."

Mira exhaled, the tight knot in her chest loosening just a bit. "Thank you, Abhay," she whispered. "I trust you completely. I just... I need to face this. I need to understand."

"You've always had incredible strength, Mira," Abhay replied, his voice filled with quiet admiration. "But remember to trust yourself too. You've got this. I'll see you tomorrow."

As she ended the call, a wave of emotions washed over her—relief, fear, and a flicker of hope. The idea of delving into her past lives, of uncovering memories buried deep within her subconscious, was a necessary step, a key to unlocking the pain she couldn't quite put into words.

Mira placed the phone down and looked out at the darkening sky. She knew this journey into her past might be painful, but with Abhay's guidance, she felt a glimmer of readiness, a small, steady flame of courage burning within her. It was time to face the shadows of her own history, to find the answers that had eluded her for so long.

The drive to Abhay's clinic was quiet, punctuated only by the hum of the car engine and the occasional rustle of leaves in the wind. Mira's mind was a swirl of anticipation and anxiety, her thoughts racing through the possibilities of what she might uncover. This wasn't her first experience with past life regression—she had guided many clients through their own journeys—but it was the first time she was stepping into this vulnerable space with the help of a professional herself. Abhay is going to witness her vulnerability. The difference between observing and experiencing felt as vast as an ocean, and she wasn't sure if she was ready to plunge into its depths.

Chapter 29

The clinic was nestled in a serene part of the city, surrounded by tall trees that offered a natural barrier from the noise of the outside world. It was a small, unassuming building, but the moment Mira stepped inside, she felt the shift. The energy was calming, a mix of sandalwood incense and the soft, ambient hum of meditative music playing in the background. Abhay had always maintained a space that felt safe, almost sacred—a sanctuary for those seeking answers from the shadows of their past.

Abhay greeted her at the door with a warm smile, his eyes crinkling at the corners. He was a tall man with a gentle demeanour, his presence exuding an aura of calm and wisdom. He led Mira to his consultation room, where soft, golden light filled the space, casting a warm glow over the muted colours of the walls. The room was furnished with a comfortable reclining chair, surrounded by shelves filled with books on psychology, spirituality, and ancient healing practices.

"Mira," he said, his voice a soothing balm, "I'm glad you're here. Are you ready for this?"

Mira nodded, though her heart was pounding in her chest. "I am," she replied softly. "But I'm also... anxious. It's different being on this side of the experience."

Abhay gave her a reassuring smile. "That's normal," he said. "But remember, this is your journey. We're not forcing anything. We'll let your subconscious guide us to whatever needs to be revealed. Just trust the process."

He gestured to her to take a seat in the reclining chair, and she settled in, feeling the soft leather cradle under her body. Abhay dimmed the lights slightly and took a seat beside her, his presence comforting and steady. He held a small metronome in his hand, a tool he often used to help clients slip into a deep, relaxed state.

"We'll start with a brief induction," Abhay explained, his voice adopting a rhythmic, calming cadence. "I want you to focus on your breathing, Mira. Inhale deeply... hold it for a moment... and exhale slowly. Let each breath guide you deeper into relaxation."

Mira followed his instructions, closing her eyes as she let her body sink into the chair. Abhay continued speaking, his voice smooth and steady, guiding her through a process known as progressive relaxation. He encouraged her to release the tension in her body, starting from her toes and moving up through her legs, torso, arms, and neck, until she felt a wave of calm wash over her.

"Now, Mira," Abhay said softly, "I want you to picture a staircase in your mind. It's a beautiful, old stone staircase, leading down into a place of safety and comfort. With each step you take, you'll feel yourself drifting deeper into relaxation, deeper into your subconscious mind."

Mira visualized the staircase, its stone steps cool and smooth under her bare feet. She took one step, then another, feeling herself sink further into a trance-like state. By the time she reached the bottom, her mind felt like it was floating, untethered from her physical body.

"You're standing at the base of the staircase now," Abhay continued. "There's a door in front of you. When you open this door, you'll step into a memory, a moment from a past life that is connected to the pain you're experiencing now. Trust what comes to you. Let the images, feelings, and sensations flow naturally."

Mira hesitated for a moment, feeling a flicker of fear. But she took a deep breath, and in her mind's eye, she pushed open the heavy wooden door. The moment she stepped through, a rush of sensations hit her like a wave—sights, sounds, even the distinct smell of the sea. She found herself standing on a cliff, overlooking a vast, churning ocean. The wind whipped her hair around her face, and she could feel the rough fabric of a simple dress against her skin.

"What do you see, Mira?" Abhay's voice came through, gentle but grounding, pulling her back to the present moment.

"I'm... by the sea," Mira whispered. "The air is salty. There's a storm brewing. I feel... sadness. A deep, aching sadness."

Abhay's voice was steady. "Look around. Who are you with? What is happening?"

Mira's vision sharpened. She turned, and there was a man standing beside her—a familiar face, yet different. It was Suraj, but not as she knew him in this lifetime. He wore simple clothing, his face weathered, his eyes filled with a mixture of love, sorrow and anger.

"It's him," she murmured, her voice tinged with disbelief. "It's Suraj, but... it's different. We're arguing. He wants me to stay, but I'm leaving. I feel trapped. I feel... betrayed."

Mira's breath hitched as the emotions from the memory flooded her. It felt real—too real. Tears slipped down her cheeks as she relived the scene, the heartbreak raw and immediate. The vision blurred, dissolving like mist. Mira's body trembled as she clutched the arms of the chair, her knuckles white.

"It's okay," Abhay soothed. "You're safe. You're here with me now. What you experienced was a glimpse of the past. It's connected to your feelings today—the unresolved betrayal, the sorrow that lingered across lifetimes."

"Take your time, Mira," Abhay said softly. "Let the memory unfold. What happens next?"

Mira swallowed hard, struggling to find her voice. "I... I walked away. I turned my back on him, even though it was breaking my heart. He called after me, begging me not to leave. But I won't stop. I couldn't." Abhay guided her softly but firmly, "go back to the same lifetime and see how you reach here."

Mira's regression session in Abhay's clinic revealed the life of Bhanumati, a woman whose story unfolded in medieval Rajasthan, during a time when art, culture, and societal structures were deeply intertwined with rigid traditions. This life gave Mira profound insights into her current struggles and

Bhanumati was born into a family of weavers in a desert village known for its vibrant textiles. From a young age, she displayed extraordinary talent, weaving intricate designs that seemed almost mystical. Her family recognized her gift but saw it only as a means to elevate their social standing. Her father, a stern man bound by societal expectations, often reminded her that her skill was valuable only as a bargaining chip for a good marriage.

Despite this, Bhanumati found joy and freedom in her craft. Weaving was her escape—a way to express the vivid dreams and visions that filled her mind. She would often stay up late under the light of an oil lamp, creating patterns inspired by the stars, the wind, and the stories of gods and goddesses told by the village elders.

However, her life changed when she turned sixteen. Her father arranged her marriage to Bhavar, a wealthy merchant from a nearby town. Bhavar was much older than Bhanumati but was captivated by her beauty and the fame her talent had brought her. To her family, this was an ideal match—a step up in status and security.

At first, Bhanumati believed she could find happiness in her new life. Bhavar treated her kindly and praised her work, commissioning her to create elaborate tapestries for his clients and trade partners. Her creations became highly sought after, bringing wealth and prestige to Bhavar's household.

But as time passed, Bhavar's demeanour changed. He began to see Bhanumati not as an individual but as an extension of his status. He dictated what she could create, often demanding mundane patterns that would sell quickly rather than the imaginative designs she loved. He forbade her from weaving anything without his approval and kept her earnings under his control.

Bhanumati's world became smaller and darker. The loom, once a symbol of freedom, now felt like a cage. Her spirit yearned to break free, but societal norms and her own fears kept her silent. She feared that defying Bhavar would bring shame to her family and leave her without protection or purpose.

One day, while visiting the village temple, Bhanumati encountered a traveling mystic named Raghvan. He was staying in the temple for a few days. His presence was magnetic, and his words stirred something deep within her. He spoke of liberation and the divine power within every soul. She started discussing all kinds of things with him. One day, seeing the sadness in her eyes, he said, "Your hands hold the power of creation, yet your silence binds your spirit. To honour the divine within you, you must create from your truth, not from fear."

His words stayed with her, awakening a spark of courage. That night, Bhanumati began weaving in secret. She poured her soul into a tapestry unlike any she had ever created—a stunning depiction of a phoenix rising from flames. The vibrant threads symbolized her suppressed dreams, her pain, and her yearning for freedom.

When Bhavar discovered the tapestry, he was furious. He accused her of defiance and destroyed the masterpiece before her eyes. The loss was devastating, but in that moment, Bhanumati realized that her silence had only given Bhavar more power. She could no longer live a life dictated by someone else.

Summoning all her courage, Bhanumati left Bhavar's home one day, carrying only her loom and a few belongings. This was the moment she saw in the beginning. She sought refuge in a nearby monastery known for its spiritual teachings and community of artisans. The monks welcomed her, recognizing her talent and her desire for liberation.

At the monastery, Bhanumati found a new purpose. She wove tapestries for the temple, each one a reflection of her spiritual awakening. Her work became an offering to the divine, free from the constraints of commerce and control. Over time, she became known as a spiritual artist, her creations inspiring others to seek their own truth.

Though she found peace in her later years, Bhanumati carried the scars of her past. She often reflected on the years she had spent in silence, wondering how her life might have been different if she had stood up for herself sooner. Yet, she also recognized that her journey had brought her to a place of profound understanding and

As Mira recounted Bhanumati's life in Abhay's clinic, she felt a deep connection to her past self. She saw how Bhanumati 's story mirrored her own struggles with suppressing her voice and creativity in the face of others' expectations. Bhanumati 's life was a lesson in the consequences of silence and the transformative power of reclaiming one's truth.

Mira also understood that her encounter with Suraj in this life was no coincidence. Suraj's controlling behaviour had triggered the same feelings of restraint and suppression that Bhanumati experienced with Bhavar. The regression showed Mira that this was her chance to break the cycle and she is ready for it.

Abhay guided Mira to release the emotional weight of Bhanumati's story, helping her see it as a source of strength rather than pain. "You are not bound by the choices of your past life," he said. "You have the power to write a new story." "Was it all real?" Mira asked

"It's not about what's real in a factual sense," Abhay explained gently. "It's about the emotional truth. Your subconscious mind holds onto patterns, traumas, and connections that transcend time. What you saw was a symbolic memory, a reflection of a deeper wound you've been carrying."

Mira nodded slowly, her mind processing the fragments of the vision. "It makes sense now," she whispered. "The pain I felt with Suraj—it wasn't just from this lifetime. It was the echo of a promise broken long ago."

Mira left the session with a renewed sense of purpose. She realized that her gift as a healer was not just about helping others but also about healing herself. Bhanumati's voice, silenced for so long, now echoed within her, urging her to live authentically.

Abhay smiled softly, reaching out to squeeze her hand. "You've taken a brave step today, Mira. Understanding the past is the first step toward healing in the present. But remember, the journey isn't over. It's just begun."

Mira gave a small, grateful smile, feeling the weight on her heart lighten just a bit. For the first time in weeks, she felt a flicker of hope—a belief that she could untangle the threads of her past and finally find the closure she needed.

Before parting, they scheduled a follow-up appointment, but it wasn't for another month. Abhay was heading abroad, conducting workshops and guiding new clients through the delicate process of past life regression. He promised Mira that when he returned, they would continue exploring the threads she had glimpsed today—going deeper, peeling back the layers of memory that held the answers she was seeking.

"I need time to process this anyway," Mira had said, attempting a smile. Abhay nodded, understanding in his eyes.

"Yes, it's best not to rush," he agreed. "The subconscious needs time to integrate what surfaced today. We'll go deeper. He paused for a moment, as if choosing his words carefully. "What you saw today wasn't just a fragment of another life. It's part of a larger story—a thread that connects to who you are now. Pay attention to how it resonates with your experiences, your relationships, and even your struggles. The past isn't meant to hold you back; it's meant to teach you, to remind you of the strength and wisdom you've carried through lifetimes."

With a small, encouraging smile, he added, "Be gentle with yourself, Mira. The journey you've started is profound, and the answers will come in their own time. Trust the process and, more importantly, trust yourself. You're uncovering not just the past but the essence of your soul."

As Mira walked out, his words stayed with her, echoing like a quiet promise of the transformations yet to come.

By the time she reached home, Mira felt a quiet peace settling within her. The past wasn't something to fear or avoid; it was a guide, a teacher, a map to her soul's evolution. And she was ready—ready to listen, to learn, and to heal.

The night was still and quiet, the faint rustle of leaves outside barely audible. Mira and Atmaj lay side by side, their breathing soft and synchronized in the sanctuary of her home. It had been about a week since Mira's first past life regression therapy session with Abhay, and though she had been deeply moved by the insights she gained, her conscious mind had since settled back into her daily life. But tonight, the veil between her subconscious and another realm seemed to thin. As Mira drifted deeper into sleep, a vivid, intricate dream began to unfold.

Mira found herself standing in a colossal temple unlike anything she had seen in her present life. The architecture was grand and otherworldly, with massive stone pillars carved with intricate patterns that seemed to shimmer faintly in the dim light of hundreds of oil lamps. The ceiling stretched high into the heavens, adorned with detailed frescoes depicting celestial beings and mystical symbols. The air was thick with the scent of incense, a mix of sandalwood, myrrh, and spices.

She looked down at herself and noticed she was wearing a long, flowing gown of deep indigo, embroidered with silver thread that glinted as she moved. The gown was heavy but regal, signifying her position as a trainee in this sacred space.

In front of her stood an imposing figure—the Priest, a man of immense power and wisdom. He wore a similar gown, though his was adorned with golden patterns and intricate designs that radiated authority. His presence was magnetic, his deep-set eyes piercing yet kind. His long, silver hair cascaded down his back, and a large amulet with an unfamiliar symbol rested on his chest. The Priest exuded a calm yet commanding energy that both awed and comforted Mira.

The temple wasn't just a place of worship—it was the centre of a vast spiritual and scholarly order. Beyond the central hall were sprawling corridors leading to libraries filled with ancient scrolls and manuscripts, meditation chambers, and an altar room bathed in golden light. This was not just a temple but a sacred institution where spiritual seekers were trained in divine knowledge, rituals, and the esoteric arts.

Mira realized that she was a part of this world. She wasn't just visiting; she belonged here. She was a disciple, one of the chosen few handpicked by the Priest himself. Her memories in the dream told her that she had been brought to this temple as a child, perhaps no older than eight or nine, to train under the Priest's guidance. Over the years, she had learned sacred chants, rituals, and the secrets of divine energy.

In the dream, her relationship with the Priest was one of deep respect and devotion. He was her mentor, her guide, and almost a father figure. Despite his stern demeanour, there was a quiet kindness in the way he taught her, correcting her mistakes with patience and encouraging her to trust her inner strength.

That night in the dream, she was standing beside him at the temple altar, assisting him in a ritual. The altar was magnificent, made of shimmering crystal and adorned with offerings of flowers, fruits, and sacred artifacts. A large, golden flame burned in the centre, radiating a warmth that seemed to resonate in her very soul.

As the Priest chanted in a language unfamiliar yet strangely comforting, Mira followed his lead, her voice blending harmoniously with his. She felt a profound connection to the ritual, as though her very existence was tied to the energy they were invoking. The flame on the altar flared brightly, illuminating the entire temple in a golden glow, and Mira felt an overwhelming sense of purpose and belonging.

But as the ritual continued, the dream began to shift. A subtle tension filled the air, and the once serene temple seemed to darken slightly. The Priest's voice grew deeper, more urgent, as though he was preparing her for something significant. He turned to her and spoke directly, his voice echoing in the vast space.

"You must remember, child," he said, his eyes locking onto hers. "Your path will not be easy. The knowledge we guard here will one day be yours to carry, but it will come at a great cost. Stay true to your light, no matter how dark the world around you may become."

Before she could respond, the scene shifted again. She was no longer in the temple but in a vast courtyard surrounded by towering palaces. The sky above was dark and stormy, and she saw herself standing alone, clutching a staff adorned with glowing crystals. The Priest was gone, and she felt a deep sense of loss and urgency. It was as though she had been left to face something immense on her own.

Mira woke up, her heart racing and her breath quick. The dream had been so vivid, so real, that it took her a moment to realize she was back in her bed, with Atmaj sleeping peacefully beside her. She sat up, her mind racing with questions. Who was the Priest? What was the temple? And why did she feel as though the dream was more than just a dream?

Chapter 30

After finishing her breakfast, Mira settled into the quiet sanctuary of her home library, the soft morning light streaming through the tall windows and glinting off the rows of books. She opened her laptop, a familiar ritual she performed twice daily, scanning through her emails with a mix of anticipation and duty. Among the usual correspondence from her publisher, a few enthusiastic fans and messages from strangers seeking guidance. Their words: heavy with longing and hope. This routine, though simple, had become a sacred part of her day—a bridge between her inner world and the countless lives she touched from afar. One of the emails was….

> Dear Mira,

I don't know if you remember me, but I came to you in 2019. At the time, I hated your advice. But after failing to make it as an artist, I took a job teaching art therapy at a local school. It wasn't what I wanted, but it brought unexpected joy and stability. Last month, one of my students' parents commissioned a series of my paintings, and now I have an exhibition next spring. You were right. Thank you.

- Subha

Mira remembered her at once. It was 3 years back.

The clock chimed softly in the corner of Mira's consultation room, its golden hands pointing to 11:00 AM. The room smelled faintly of lavender and sage, a delicate attempt to soothe even the most sceptical visitors. Across the table sat Subha, a 27-year-old with coloured green hair and dark brown eyes that burned with ambition.

"I want to know if my career as an artist will flourish," Subha said, her voice tight with hope. Her fingers nervously traced the rim of her coffee cup.

Mira shuffled her cards with practiced ease, feeling the energy settle. "Art will be your path," she said after a moment, her voice calm and measured. "But not now. You'll need to take a detour—work with children, perhaps in teaching or therapy. That experience will lead you to success in ways you don't yet understand."

Subha's face hardened. "Teaching? Therapy? That's not my dream. I don't want to babysit kids; I want to paint!" She stood abruptly, nearly knocking over her chair. "Thanks, but no thanks."

The session ended with Subha leaving in a huff, her critique of Mira muttered under her breath as she slammed the door.

Three years later, Mira received this email.

Mira smiled softly, her fingers hovering over the reply button.

In the same line, a few weeks before, her meeting with Kavita was very satisfying. She still remembered how Kavita felt cheated on their first meeting of tarot card reading sessions.

Kavita, a sharply dressed woman with piercing eyes, tapped her pen impatiently as Mira laid out the cards.

"My business is stagnating," Kavita said bluntly. "What should I do to turn things around?"

Mira studied the spread before her. "Expand into wellness products," she said simply.

Kavita laughed, a sharp, dismissive sound. "Wellness? I sell tech gadgets, not incense sticks." "You'll face resistance at first, even from yourself," Mira continued, unfazed. "But by late 2023, wellness tech will be a growing trend. Trust me. "Kavita stood, brushing non-existent lint off her blazer. "I don't think you understand my business. Thanks for the entertainment."

A few weeks back, Mira received a call.

"I'd like to meet," Kavita said. Her voice was quieter than Mira remembered, almost sheepish.

Over tea in a bustling café, Kavita confessed. "A few months after I saw you, my company nearly collapsed. Desperate, I took a risk and launched a wellness gadget line. It's now our best-selling product. I'm sorry I doubted you."

Mira smiled gently. "Sometimes the path we resist the most is the one we need the most."

As Mira reflected on these moments, she realized something profound: her role was not to be understood in the moment but to plant seeds that would bloom in their own time. Her clients' gratitude, though delayed, reaffirmed her faith in her gift.

Each message, email, and meeting reminded her that truth often unfolds quietly, in the spaces between resistance and realization. And in those moments, Mira found her own purpose renewed.

The storm raged outside, its howling winds and relentless rain a symphony of chaos. Mira lay on her bed, the dim light of her room flickering as if in tune with the storm's unrest. An odd energy permeated the air, thick and electric, making her skin prickle. Strange sounds echoed from the darkness beyond her window—whispers, perhaps, or merely the storm's tricks.

Mira closed her eyes, drawing slow, deliberate breaths to centre herself. The world outside faded, but the peculiar pull within her grew stronger, like invisible hands guiding her mind. Without moving a muscle, she surrendered to the urge.

Her tarot deck, resting untouched on the bedside table, seemed to awaken. In her mind's eye, she spread the cards effortlessly, her inner vision as clear as if she were holding them. She asked the question that lingered in the depths of her heart: what do you want to tell me?

Though she knew the risks of reading for oneself, she embraced the moment from a place of detached awareness—a witness state free from bias. In this stillness, answers began to take shape.

Chapter 31

As Mira's mind attuned to the cards and the question she had asked, an extraordinary shift began. The dense, storm-laden air of her room seemed to dissolve, replaced by a luminous, surreal stillness. She felt herself being pulled—not physically, but energetically—into a realm vastly different from the familiar dimensions of her earthly experience.

This place vibrated with a frequency so high it felt almost musical, as if existence itself was composed of harmonics. Colours beyond the earthly spectrum shimmered in the space, each hue pulsing with life and intelligence. The air was not empty; it carried an unspoken language, a symphony of thoughts and messages that bypassed words, resonating directly within her being.

Structures, if they could be called that, formed and dissolved in fluid motions, more like light sculptures than solid matter. Beings were present, though they had no defined forms—only radiant fields of energy, pulsating with love, wisdom, and a profound neutrality.

Mira realized she was in a dimension far beyond the density of the physical or even the astral—a plane of pure consciousness, perhaps the 5th dimension or higher. Here, dualities blurred; time stretched and folded in ways her earthly mind could barely grasp. She felt connected to everything—every thought, every being, every possibility—yet entirely separate, observing it all with a calm clarity.

In this elevated state, the answer to her question began to take shape, not as words or images, but as a deep, all-encompassing knowing. The path ahead wasn't linear; it was a web of potential, each thread shimmering with its own energy, waiting for her to choose how to weave her story.

Her cards were alive. She started going towards a big figure of Time Whisperer card. She entered that card as if it was a portal to go where she ruled as a Time Whisperer, custodian of timeless knowledge. She was a bridge between eras, with an innate ability to tap into the essence of forgotten pasts and unveil potential futures. Her role often involves preserving the wisdom of time while guiding others toward clarity and enlightenment. She could listen to the echoes of time—emotional imprints left by events or souls. This could include understanding the significance of choices, the weight of regrets, and the fulfilment of lessons carried across lifetimes.

Time was not linear for her anymore; it's a vast, multidimensional realm. She was moving seamlessly through its folds, aligning spiritual, emotional, and cosmic elements.

She was helping others reconcile with unresolved pasts or fears of the future. By unlocking these hidden truths, she was able to assist in emotional and spiritual healing, so souls around there could find their true purpose. Atmosphere around her started changing and another card emerged in front of her. She entered it with ease as if she was not walking but gliding into it. Beautiful card with the blooming lotuses, the crescent moon, and the celestial figure radiating with creation.

 At first, Mira was overwhelmed by the suddenness of the thought. She placed her hand instinctively on her abdomen, feeling a warmth that seemed to emanate from her body. The notion of creating something so intimate and profound filled her heart with an overwhelming sense of purpose. At the same time, questions arose: Am I ready for this?

Mira looked down and saw her body transformed. Her belly was rounded, full, and glowing with a radiant golden light that seemed to ripple outward like gentle waves. She placed her hands on the curve, and a warmth spread from her palms, connecting her deeply to the life growing inside her. Her entire being radiated a sense of divine beauty and purpose.

She was a vessel of creation, carrying within her something extraordinary, something cosmic. The stars around her seemed to dance in celebration, recognizing her as part of the eternal cycle of life.

Her room, the ethereal glow of the vision, began to fade, replaced by the dim, familiar light of her bedside lamp. She lied back against the pillows, her breathing slow but her mind racing. Her hand instinctively moved to her belly, the memory of its rounded fullness in the vision still vivid. Her fingers linger there, and an electric thought pierces through her—I am seven days late.

Her heart skipped a beat as reality sunk in. A tear slipped down her cheek, not from fear or sadness, but from the overwhelming weight of the unknown. She whispered softly into the darkness, "If this is true, I'm ready."

As the first light of dawn begins to seep into her room, Mira rose slowly, the anticipation swirling within her, ready to face the truth that the morning would bring.

She was to travel to Atmaj's hometown to attend a havan conducted in his home. After puja and havan she was still processing the grandeur of the havan ceremony as she settled into the guest room in Atmaj's family home. The house was magnificent—its vastness almost overwhelming, filled with the warmth of tradition and the care of a loving family. But exhaustion had begun to weigh her down, both from the day's activities and the toll of her early pregnancy. She had kept her secret, hesitant to reveal it just yet, especially amidst the formality and significance of the event.

Mira was pulled from her sleep by a faint knocking sound. For a moment, she forgot where she was, her heart pounding as she tried to orient herself. Then she remembered—she was in Karwar, in Atmaj's family home.

The knocking persisted. "Who's there?" she called softly, her voice trembling slightly.

"It's me," came a familiar voice, steady and warm.

Relief flooded through her as she recognized Atmaj's voice. She opened the door to find him standing there, his face lit up with a wide smile.

Without a word, he stepped inside, closing and locking the door behind him. Before she could say anything, he pulled her into a tight embrace. His warmth and scent enveloped her, chasing away the lingering remnants of her exhaustion.

"I couldn't sleep," he murmured, his lips close to her ear. "I kept thinking of you, wondering if you were okay."

"I'm fine," she replied, her voice soft but unsteady. "Just tired."

Atmaj's eyes were full of love and desires. He started guiding her toward the bed, his arms around her waist. Mira felt his tenderness in every gesture, his desire tempered with care. Atmaj gently pushed her back onto the bed, his hands supporting her as she lay down. The softness of the mattress cradled her body, but it was his touch—steady and loving—that made her feel truly safe. Atmaj pulled back for a moment, his hand resting on her cheek. "Are you okay?" he asked, his voice tender. Mira nodded, a small smile playing on her lips. "I'm okay," she whispered. As he leaned in again, their movements became fluid, a silent language spoken through touch and closeness.

As their intimacy deepened, Atmaj became increasingly attuned to Mira's body, noticing the subtle but undeniable changes in her. His hands moved instinctively over her curves, lingering on the fullness of her breasts and the roundness of her hips. He pressed himself closer, feeling the tightness of her body as they moved together in perfect rhythm.

Mira's body trembled as Atmaj's passion surged, his movements becoming more intense, driven by the undeniable connection between them. His hands roamed her body with fervour, his touch lingering on the fullness of her breasts. His breath hissed as he realized just how much they had changed. "You are so perfect, Mira,' he murmured between heavy breaths, his voice filled with awe and desire. His hands squeezed her breasts gently but firmly, marvelling at their newfound softness and size.

As their movements became more synchronized, Atmaj's voice grew louder, his pleasure spilling into the air in unrestrained cries. He whispered soft, romantic words between his gasps. "You are mine, Mira, my everything. You drive me crazy. I love you so much."

It was as if he had been starving for this connection. His lips and tongue were exploring every inch of her sensitive skin. He was alternating between gentle sucks and firmer pulls. His teeth grazed her lightly just enough to make her gasp. His hands kneaded the fullness of her breasts as his mouth worked tirelessly. His passion intensified with every passing moment. You are incredible. I can't get enough of you. He murmured between kisses. "You are perfect." Mira moaned softly. The sensitivity of her body, heightened by her pregnancy, made every touch, every flick of his tongue feel electric. She arched her back, pressing herself closer to him. Surrendering to the overwhelming pleasure he was giving her. Atmar's hunger only seemed to grow. He moved from one breast to the other, lavishing equal attention on each. His tongue circled her nipple before pulling it into his mouth again. His hands continued to explore her, sliding from her waist to her hips and in between thighs. "You taste like heaven," he whispered against her skin. His voice hoarse with desire. I could stay here forever.

"You are so sensitive," he murmured. His fingers circled her devil's teat, in slow, deliberate motions, applying just enough pressure to make her body tremble beneath him. As Mira's breaths grew heavier, Atmaj's movements became more confident. He alternated between gentle circles and firmer strokes, finding a rhythm that matched her responses. Her moans filled the room, soft at first, but growing louder as waves of pleasure rippled through her body. "I love how you respond to me, how you trust me with every part of you," he whispered. "Atmaj," she gasped, her voice trembling with both pleasure and emotion. Don't stop, he smiled against her skin, his lips pressing soft kisses to her inner thighs. "I won't dream of it," he said, his voice filled with both passion and tenderness. As his touch intensified, Mira's body arched. Her fingers tangled in his hair as he brought her closer and closer to the peak of pleasure. Atmaj's focus never wavered, his movements precise yet filled with love. When she finally reached her climax, her entire body shuddered, her moans echoed in the quiet of the room. Atmaj held her steady, his hands gentle as he continued to touch her, drawing out her pleasure for as long as possible.

The room was cloaked in a gentle twilight, the only illumination coming from the faint glow of the moon filtering through the sheer curtains. Mira lay entwined in Atmaj's arms, their breaths still harmonizing after the passionate crescendo that had drawn them closer than ever before. The world outside seemed distant, irrelevant, as if only this moment existed.

Atmaj brushed a stray lock of hair from Mira's face, his touch lingering on her cheek. His eyes, deep and tender, searched hers as if trying to uncover the secret she was holding within. "What is it?" he asked softly, his voice still husky. "There's something in your eyes… something you're not saying."

Mira chuckled quietly, the sound of a melody that made his chest tighten. She turned onto her side, her fingers tracing lazy patterns on his chest, feeling the steady beat of his heart beneath her touch. "Atmaj," she began, her tone teasing but warm, "do you remember how you told me this house holds all your most cherished memories?"

He nodded, a faint smile tugging at his lips. "Of course. Every corner has a story, every wall a part of me."

She leaned in closer, her voice dropping to a whisper. "Well… it's about to hold another memory. One that will change everything."

He froze, his brow furrowing slightly. "Mira, what are you—"

She silenced him with a finger to his lips, her own trembling with a smile that was too full of emotion to hide. "I'm saying," she whispered, her eyes glistening, "that there's a tiny heartbeat starting inside me. Atmaj… I'm pregnant."

For a moment, there was only silence. His breath hitched, his eyes widening as the meaning of her words sank in. "You… Mira, are you serious?" His voice was barely audible, as if he was afraid speaking too loudly would shatter the moment.

She nodded, tears of joy slipping down her cheeks. "Yes. It's real. We're going to have a baby."

Atmaj stared at her, his face a mixture of disbelief, joy, and awe. Then, like a wave breaking over him, reality hit, and he pulled her close, his arms wrapping around her tightly. He buried his face in her hair, his voice shaking with emotion. "Mira… I don't know how to describe this. I—" He broke off, his laughter mingling with tears. "A baby… our baby."

Mira laughed softly, her fingers threading through his hair as she held him. "You're going to be a father, Atmaj. Can you believe it?"

He pulled back slightly, cradling her face in his hands as if she were the most precious thing in the universe. "You… you've given me everything, Mira. I thought I knew what happiness was, but this… this is something else entirely."

They lay there, wrapped in each other, the weight of the moment sinking in. Atmaj rested his hand on her stomach, his touch reverent. "Our star," he murmured. "Our little universe, growing here."

Mira nodded, her tears flowing freely now, her heart full. "Our love, Atmaj. Made real."

The room was full—of dreams, of hope, of a future they could now see more clearly than ever. Above them, the moon continued its watch, as if blessing this sacred beginning of a new chapter in their lives.

Chapter 32

The gentle morning light streamed through the curtains, filling the room with warmth. Mira stretched lazily in bed, her hand instinctively reaching out for Atmaj, who was already up. She heard the rhythmic sound of his breathing exercises from the terrace, a routine he had perfected over the years. A faint smile played on her lips as she listened to the steady inhale and exhale, a melody of vitality and mindfulness.

Their families, once hesitant, now celebrated their union wholeheartedly. The elders remarked on how Mira and Atmaj brought out the best in each other, their connection undeniable and inspiring. Their marriage had become a symbol of growth, resilience, and love for everyone in their lives.

Their house had become a haven, a space filled with love, creativity, and harmony. Every corner reflected their shared journey: Mira's tarot deck, neatly arranged on her desk, symbols of her ever-expanding spiritual work, and Atmaj's minimalist running gear by the door, a testament to his thriving work as a breatharian and endurance runner. Together, they had found not just a home, but a sanctuary where their souls could grow.

Mira had completely embraced her calling as a healer, her work gaining even more recognition after her bestselling book Time Whisperer. Invitations to festivals, podcasts, and workshops poured in, but she chose her commitments carefully, valuing the balance she and Atmaj had cultivated. Her connection to the cosmos felt deeper than ever, her readings and healings now infused with a contentment and clarity she'd never known before.

Atmaj, too, was thriving. His discipline as a breatharian—one who nourishes himself through pranic energy—had transformed into a mission to inspire others. He combined this with his love of running, conducting workshops and retreats that blended breath control, energy optimization, and endurance. People marvelled at his ability to run ultramarathons with seemingly boundless energy, becoming a beacon of what the human body and spirit could achieve when in harmony with the universe.

Chapter 33

Under a clear, starry Bangalore sky, Mira and Atmaj sat on their terrace, the quiet night embracing their newfound joy. Mira rested her hands tenderly on her growing belly, a soft smile illuminating her face as she looked at Atmaj. His eyes, full of warmth and pride, met hers as he held her hand, their silent connection speaking volumes. Around them lay open books, a notepad with hastily written ideas, and a cozy spread of blankets, all symbols of their eager planning for the new life they were bringing into the world. It was a moment of pure commitment, shared joy, and the anticipation of a future that already felt brighter under the expanse of the glittering sky.

"It is like living a dream." Atmaj said, pulling Mira into his arms. "But the real beauty is sharing this dream with you." Mira was beaming with joy.

Their foreheads touched, and for a moment, they stayed still, their hearts beating as one. Slowly, his lips sought hers, and they shared a kiss so tender, so profound, that it seemed to carry the promise of their future. Mira's hand rested on his chest, feeling the steady rhythm of his breath.

Atmaj's hand gently caressed the curve of her belly, a silent acknowledgment of the life they had created. With each kiss, each touch, they wove their dreams into reality, their love flowing like a river—deep, unyielding, and eternal.

9 7 9 8 8 8 9 6 3 2 1 2 8 6